Too Old
for Murder

by

BETTY INMAN SHORTT

Dedication

Too Old for Murder is dedicated to my dear friend, Joyce, who is no longer with us. She was fun, quirky and sassy. She often used spicy language, and did not always conform to conventional dress codes.

We met at Missouri State University, where we were invariably the oldest people in the room. Our love of literature and writing put us in a lot of the same classes.

Over the years, we became the best of friends. She would help me if I needed it, and I would return the favor.

Sadly, Joyce was diagnosed with Parkinson's, and eventually had to leave Springfield to live with her son in California. Occasionally, we talked on the phone, but it became difficult for her. The last time I talked to her, I said, "Joyce, I am going to write a book and make you the main character. She was so pleased.

God bless you Joyce. This is for you. I hope you enjoy my interpretation of your personality. You were special.

Acknowledgments

I would like to thank Jack Merritt, our former Greene County Sheriff, for his advice on guns, witness protection, and which branch of law enforcement is responsible for what. Jack and his wife, Wanda, are longtime friends, and schoolmates of mine. They have been very helpful and supportive.

You will see, however, I have played fast and loose with police procedures. That is on me, not Jack.

I hope you enjoy what I have written, even if it's not exactly how things would go down. My attempt at humor got in the way.

I want to thank my son, Mark, who read the first nineteen pages, and loved it so much, he refused to read anymore until it was complete. He wanted to read it from beginning to end, so he didn't get lost in the process. He has encouraged me to get a move on, and make it to the finish line.

My sister, Beverly Lolley, has been with me all the way. She has read it in bits and pieces as it developed, and offered useful advice along the way. I really appreciate you, Bev.

Also, I want to say thanks to my daughter, Sarah Shelburn, Nancy Daily, and Candy Simonson for their help with the cover. I drew the ladies, as I saw them, but they put the pieces together.

Contents

Chapter 1

My name is Joyce Greenly. I'm 72 and live in a retirement facility, not because I have to, but hell, I've got the money, hate cleaning, cooking, and doing laundry, so why not? Domestic duties were never my forte. My two sons live in France and were delighted to see me make the move. They think my eccentric tendencies will be tamed in The White Dove.

They have no idea how wrong they are.

Bam! Bam! Bam! It was six-ten a.m. as my door bounced on its hinges. I had barely turned the knob, when my friend, Gertrude, burst into the room and grabbed my shoulders. Her grey hair had come loose from its usual tight bun, and the front of her pink jogging suit pumped up and down as she struggled to catch her breath.

"Joyce! Jake is dead. I...I mean he's been killed!" she shouted in ragged gasps.

"Where? What happened?" I asked in a softer but concerned voice in an effort to inspire her to turn down the volume. Gertrude can't hear an elephant fart, and I've never been able to convince her how loud she talks.

"He's in the gazebo with a knife in his back. Joyce, come

with me NOW! You always know what to do. It's so awful," she yelled. "I walked over to say good morning to him. I got closer, and started to speak, and realized his eyes were wide open. His jaw had dropped, and his dentures were about to fall out. Oh! That picture is seared into my brain. I almost fainted," she said, grabbing my shoulder for support.

"Calm down, Gert. I'll go with you. Poor Jake. This is terrible! We need to call the police, but I'm going to take my cell phone and call 911 from there. I'd like to take a good look around before the police rope us out. They might miss something that would look out of place to us, but not to them. Besides, they often act as though old people are dispensable." We can't help it if gravity takes over and our cheeks, breasts, etc. began to go south, I thought. It does not take away from our value. They'll understand someday when their body turns eighty, and their mind is still twenty.

We left my place and hurried down the sidewalk. Each person has his or her own cottage. Jake's was on our way to the gazebo. His blinds were closed. I checked his door with my hand wrapped in the tail of my shirt. It was locked. A pot of purple pansies lay on its side...not like him. Jake was as neat as a pin.

"Joyce, who would want him dead?" Gertrude yelled. "He was such a sweet man."

"Shhh," I said, holding my finger in front of my lips. "We don't want everyone up and in the middle of this."

My watch showed six-fifteen. Breakfast is served at seven. Most of the residents stay inside until a few minutes before the food is on the buffet. Then they walk, waddle and limp to the main building. A few of us more spry seniors go for early walks: for the most part Jake, Gertrude, and me.

"I don't see anyone," Gert said, in a lower but pissy tone.

"You will if you keep yelling," I answered in the same tenor.

Here we go again, I thought, as the two of us walked along, only this time it's a friend. Much different. Before retiring, my official title was 'secretary' for a private investigator. My unofficial title was, Assistant Investigator, or maybe Lead Investigator might have been more appropriate. My boss, Jim, hadn't hired me to investigate, but I could never rein in my nosey, curious tendencies. After a bit, Jim realized that I did seem to have a knack for it. My duties still included typing, but he slowly began to run some of his cases by me and ask what my thoughts were. I was thrilled, of course. Intrigue is like catnip to me: always has been. After retirement, nothing changed. My eyes and ears are always open. For some reason, things seemed to just fall in my lap. A curse or a blessing? I don't know.

We passed the last cottage and turned onto a sidewalk that led to the gazebo. Beyond it rested a small lake, edged with an occasional white flowering shrub.

From a distance, Jake appeared to be relaxing with his head

against a post. Up close, it was ugly. Jake was the "dandy" of the White Dove Retirement Center. He always showed up in freshly pressed clothes, hair combed and clean-shaven. Women swarmed after him. At the moment, stubble sprouted from his chin and his mouth gaped open. His eyes bulged and his teeth sat at an odd angle. A few threads on his shirt showed the loss of a button. It's hard to look at a good friend in this condition, and know he would be mortified that people were seeing him in such a state. Damn! Life can be cruel.

With glistening eyes, Gert pointed a trembling finger toward a large knife protruding from Jake's back. She shuddered and turned away.

"Yes, I see it. Let's not get too close. We don't want to disturb something the police might need as evidence, or leave anything to make us look like suspects. Since we are calling it in, it wouldn't be unusual to leave a fingerprint. Just the same, don't touch anything," I ordered. "Watch the corner of the last cottage, and let me know if anyone is coming. Scream, faint or yell, so it will look like we just got here."

"Why do I have to do it?" Gert said, with a frown. She folded her arms across her chest and stuck out her lower lip.

"Damn it! I can't look at Jake and check the scene if I have to watch for someone coming around the corner. Do you want to help me or not?" I barked.

"You're so bossy," she said, holding back tears.

She wasn't far from wrong. Crime scenes get my dander up.

I circled the gazebo and looked carefully at the ground and Jake. His shoes had dew on them, which told me he'd probably spent most of the night here, and it explained why he had on his regular dress clothes, and not his usual morning exercise clothing. A couple sprigs of grass, attached to a small piece of dirt lay on the first step. It wasn't hard to see where it had been torn from the lawn a few inches away. The grass displayed faint footprints in the dew near the path—something to remember. The marks would be gone soon. The sun rose higher in the sky. A few thin black scuffmarks showed on the sidewalk. Hell's bells. What had happened here?

I forced myself to give Jake a closer look. A dark ring showed around his neck, just above his collar. His knuckles were scraped and his shirt dotted with blood. His, or someone else's? It appeared he hadn't gone down without a fight. Was he strangled to death and the knife just insurance, or did it reveal the hate and anger of his killer? I couldn't imagine anyone hating the Jake we knew, but someone certainly wanted him dead.

There was very little blood around the knife wound. Putting myself in "Matlock" mode, it seemed this must mean he was dead before he was stabbed. How odd. Was he killed here or in his cottage? If he was already dead, why would someone drag him out here? The tracks and marks on the concrete made me wonder.

As I reached for my phone to call 911, I caught a glimpse of something shiny under the bench where Jake was propped.

"Look Gert, I said, louder than I would have liked, but she needed to hear me. "There's something under there." I put my cell back in my pocket. Gert left her lookout position, and we crouched as low as our slightly used bodies would allow. Both of us stared between the boards behind Jake's legs.

"What is that?"

"Looks to me like a stick pin in the shape of a snake. It has some kind of shiny stone for an eye. Wonder if it was Jake's or the killer's? Take a good look, Gert. We may not get to see it again. It may be important."

Oh, Lord! It was so hard not to grab my phone and take a bunch of pictures, but memories of a case with my old employer stopped me. It was common for a P.I. to take pictures of cheating spouses, but once when the victim's family hired Jim to work a murder case, things went all wrong. Within a few days we narrowed down a good suspect. We took a ton of pictures of the guy, his buddies, his comings and goings. Several showed him being all cozy with people he swore he didn't know from shit.

We worked with the police, even though they were not thrilled to have us. Then some butthead clerk at their headquarters let it slip we had pictures that didn't look good for the guy. The info trickled down to our killer, and only the fast use of the office thirty-eight kept us alive and rendered him dead. I took my finger off the camera button on my phone. I couldn't put Gert in that kind of danger.

Satisfied we'd seen all there was to see, I dialed 911. "My Lord, my Lord!" I yelled into the phone. "We just found our friend in the gazebo at the White Dove Retirement Center. He looks dead. Oh! Come quick, please!" I laid it on thick to make us sound as innocent as lambs. We actually were, except for the delay in reporting, but you never know how things can be perceived. After giving them our names and the address, they wanted me to stay on the line, but I feigned confusion, loss of hearing and hung up. I had better things to do than listen to comforting words from a dispatcher.

While waiting for the sound of sirens, we continued our survey of the area, and still kept an eye open for anyone who might come around the corner. We had pretty well inspected Jake and the gazebo already, so we checked the grounds further out. Faint tracks showed in the dew toward the lake, but it was hard to tell if they were made by a human, or one of the poop-filled geese that share our habitat. I didn't see any of the stinky presents they leave for us, but maybe in a rare moment this one didn't have to relieve itself. Nasty things! If it were up to me, I'd feed them all to the homeless. It would help them and help us. I'm tired of cleaning that crap off my shoes.

"Joyce, is there something beside that bush?" Gert pointed to a shrub where the trail in the dew disappeared.

"Yeah, I think you're right, but I can't see if it's a stick, dead bird, or what at this distance."

Just then we heard sirens screaming toward us.

"Dang it. Maybe we can check it out later if the police don't see it. We don't want them to arrive while we're out there. They need to think we're just reporting a body, not snooping.

As I turned toward Gertrude, over her shoulder I could see a large figure peering through the fence near the waterfall. How long had he been there? Not long, because we surely would have seen him. Wouldn't we?

I had no doubt, even at this distance who it was: Jim Landis. It was impossible not to recognize the giant of a man. He was six foot eight, and as bald as a billiard ball. He was the resident handyman, but I'd never seen him on the outside of the fence before. Why was he there now? It gave me chills for some reason, but we had no time to discuss it. I'd tell Gertrude later.

Chapter 2

We stepped to the ground beside the gazebo, put on our sweet, concerned little old lady faces, and wrapped our arms around each other. In less than three minutes we found ourselves surrounded by a swarm of cops. A few moments later the entire population of the White Dove tried to join us. They, however, could not get closer than the yellow tape, which had already been placed at the turn in the sidewalk, and out to the fence at the waterfall. Damn, that was fast!

Management, after seeing what had happened on their watch, tried in great haste to convince the residents to calm down and come have cinnamon buns and coffee. A scant few took them up on it, mostly the half blind and the 'walker' people. Crap! I wanted to go, but uniforms blocked me.

Mr. Bennett, Director of our facility, was hurrying toward us alongside a tall, lanky Springfield, MO, police officer. Mr. Bennett was pasty white, even lighter than his usual pale complexion. The cop was too thin for my taste, and young enough to make me feel old. I gave him a few points for the uniform.

Introductions were made. We learned we would be talking to Officer Scott.

"Mrs. Greenly?" he said, looking at me.

"Yes." Gert was behind me with a tight grip on my shirt.

"Are you the one who found the deceased and called in?"

"I called, but Gertrude found him first. She came and got me." I took Gert's hand from my shirt and stepped aside. I was speaking above my normal volume, so she wouldn't miss anything. She gave me a dirty look as the officer moved in front of her.

"Okay, Gertrude Bush, is that right?" he said, looking at his notes. "Let's start from the beginning. Why were you out here so early?"

"Jake...good…yes…morning…oh, no."

Gertrude is usually an articulate woman, but she visibly shook and stumbled over her words like a doped-up wino. The officer's jaw tightened, and his pen tapped on his pad as he waited for something besides the gibberish coming from her mouth.

She started again.

"I—walk. Joyce and J-Jake too. Morning nice—early—but nice. I around corner. Saw. Oh, my!"

I took her arm and patted her hand, hoping to bring some comfort, and unravel her twirling thoughts and tongue.

For my efforts, I got, "She talk," and her index finger in my ribs.

Damn! I'm sure he probably thought she had dementia.

I turned to the bewildered Officer Scott. He looked somewhat relieved. He nodded his approval, and I proceeded to tell all I knew of the morning's events. Of course, I left out our detective work. Gertrude managed a syllable here and a nod there. What a help she was! What the hell! She'd dragged me away from my morning coffee into this mess and then snapped shut like a clam. I wished at this point she had just called 911 and then come to get me. No. That's not true. Being very upset about Jake, and my nature being what it is, I would have been pissed to lose out on a chance to snoop. Suck it up, Joyce.

After delivering my account of what happened, Officer Scott said, "You can go for now, but both of you stay at your place, Mrs. Greenly. We might need to ask you some further questions. Don't repeat anything you saw or know about the case. Thank you, and I'm sorry for the loss of your friend."

We hurried past several other officers checking the scene, and ducked under the yellow tape. The coast was mostly clear now, as the residents had tired of standing around, and figured they had seen all they were going to be allowed to see. Besides, breakfast was being served, and they would have lots to talk about between bites of sweet rolls, eggs and oatmeal.

"Gertrude, what in God's name happened to you?" I asked when we were out of earshot.

"Don't start on me," she whined. "I'm not used to things like this!"

I pulled her into my cottage, closed the door and said, "You think I deal with dead bodies on a daily basis? If you're going to fall apart just telling your story, we'd better leave this to the police and hope they will give it their best shot."

Gert dropped her petite body into my favorite chair. She looked pale and said nothing. Her eyes sparkled with tears. I'd never seen her like this: weepy eyes and all. Even though I was somewhat annoyed, it was impossible not to feel sorry for her. Maybe I had been a little harsh. Just a bit, perhaps…maybe.

"How about a cup of tea?"

She nodded.

I filled two cups with water and stuck them in the microwave, gathered up a couple of tea bags, the sugar bowl, bagels, and the butter dish. A cookie sheet served as a tray for the tea items. I'd broken my nice wooden tray over the head of the guilty party in my last escapade. It can get expensive poking around in other people's business. I stopped at the fridge door and added 'tray' to my shopping list.

"Here, maybe this will help." I put the cookie sheet on the coffee table and sat in my second most favorite chair. "Want sugar in your tea? Butter on your bagel?"

She nodded in agreement to both.

I stirred sugar in her tea, buttered her bagel and handed them to her. After doing the same for myself, I leaned back against my chair. Gertrude had not moved. It was obvious my friend was very sad and shaken.

"You thought a lot of Jake, didn't you?"

"Yes." Her lips wobbled, and a tear skated down her cheek.

"I didn't realize how much," she said. "It all hit me when I tried to tell the officer. I don't mean I was in love with him. He had too many lady friends for a serious relationship, but he was a special friend. I'll miss him." She wiped her eyes on the sleeve of her pink striped shirt.

Me, too," I confessed. "He kept us all feeling sixteen. That's hard to give up. Dang it! We've got to pull it together and figure out who would have done such a horrible thing. Did he ever talk about any relatives or people he knew away from here?"

"He had a niece, but she's all I know about. He'd outlived all his siblings and never had any children of his own."

"How about the niece? Do you remember her name or where she lives?"

Gert pulled on a loose strand of hair that had fallen on her cheek. "I don't know. Seems like her name started with a 'B'. Barbara, Bonnie, something like that. She lives in Springfield. I'm pretty sure about that, but that's all I know." Her eyes stared at mine like a lost pup. The bagel lay untouched on her plate. "I'm not much help," she said.

"It's better than nothing," I said with a grin. "Maybe we can sneak a peek at Jake's file in the office. Fannie owes me one. They should have his next of kin listed. This will be the talk of the facility, so we need to keep our eyes and ears open. He may have told other people things he didn't share with us."

Gert perked up and leaned closer. In a voice, which was

loud, but almost a whisper for Gertrude, she said, "You suppose he had something of value in his place? That pin looked expensive."

We're not sure the pin was Jake's. I never saw it, or anything that looked expensive in his place. He never talked about his finances. But I did get the feeling he wasn't hurting for money. Always wore nice clothes, but who knows? Some people live beyond their means, and others wear rags and hoard every penny. He used to be an investment banker and traveled the world, so he could have more contacts and enemies than we could imagine or investigate. Holy crap, we've got a lot of digging to do."

This was depressing. It might be out of my league, not that that would stop me. Hell, it's better to turn over hundreds of stones and find nothing, than step over one with a tiny clue.

"Gert, I couldn't tell you earlier, because the police were just getting here, but I saw Big Jim Landis outside the fence staring at us just before they came around the corner. I don't know how long he had been there, and I can't imagine why he was there. It may not mean anything, but he gives me the creeps. Have you ever seen him work outside the fence?"

The doorbell rang. Gert jumped to her feet and dropped her tea. It landed on the floor with a crash. Ignoring the clutter, I went to open the door. A tall man in a dark suit stood on the porch. His stature made it obvious he was a person of authority. Gert stood cautiously just behind and to the side of me; this was becoming a habit.

"I'm Detective Lancaster," he said, showing us his badge. "You are Mrs. Greenly and Mrs. Bush? Is that correct?"

"Yes," we answered, nodding like two aging bobble heads.

"I'm Mrs. Greenly, and this is Mrs. Bush," I said, pulling Gert up beside me.

"Have either of you ladies seen this before?"

The snake pin's red eye gleamed in the morning sun. We stared intently through the small plastic bag in his hand.

"What is it?" I asked, trying to avoid a direct answer.

"A piece of the puzzle, we think. Did you ever see Mr. Robards wear it?"

Thank goodness he worded it like that. I'm not a saint, but lying to police detectives is not wise. "I never saw him with it on. How about you, Gertrude?" I asked.

"Me neither," she answered truthfully.

"How about on someone else?" he asked.

We both looked blank and shook our heads. I could feel sweat trickling down my back, and between my boobs.

"Okay, that's all for now, but if you should remember anything that might be helpful, give me a call. Here's my card. I would appreciate even the slightest thing you might remember. You can leave your cabin now, if you want. We have your phone numbers if we need anything else. Don't mention the pin to anyone," he ordered.

"Okay," we agreed. Each of us took one of his cards, closed

the door, and breathed huge sighs of relief.

"Holy crap! That was a close one," I said, beating Gertrude to my favorite chair. What the hell? It's my furniture. I needed comfort. My fiery red dye job would be turning grey if this kept up.

Gert looked a little confused, but sat in the other chair. "Do you suppose, technically, that could be classified as a lie?" she asked.

"Well, in my book, no. We never saw Jake wear that pin. We answered his second question, not the first. Besides, they can't prove we saw it. And it might not have anything to do with Jake. It could have been there for days."

We sat quietly for a few minutes trying to justify my theory about our semi-lie. Noticing the broken cup and puddle of tea, I got up to clean the floor.

Gert broke the silence a few minutes later. "Yes, but you do consider it evidence don't you?" she said, with a "not-so-fast-there-sister" stare.

I swear, she is so straight-laced, it's a wonder we're such good friends!

"You bet I do. Until proven otherwise. It's all we've got, but I may be wrong. It may have nothing to do with the case." I swept up the broken cup and put it in the trash.

"About Jim. Have you ever seen him outside the fence?"

'No, but I don't know that he doesn't go out there. Can't imagine why though. The gardener takes care of the grass or weeds on that side."

"May not be anything. Just startled me, but we do have to consider everyone until we check them out."

"You go right ahead. I've already had enough," Gert said, looking at the floor.

"Why don't we go to the dining room? I'm sure everyone is talking about what happened. Maybe someone will say something we can use. Get those hearing aids out of your pocket and in your ears. I tell you no one can see them. You need to use them if you're going to be any help."

Gertrude made a face, but pulled a little bag out of her pocket and fixed her ears. They weren't perfect, but a big improvement. Hearing aids in place, we headed to the main building. We passed between the two gray pillars that held the façade of the building. It sported a huge white dove that flew forever, but got nowhere. The automated door opened and we entered.

Chapter 3

The front lobby buzzed with noisy voices. The commotion slowed to the level of a salted slug as the news we'd arrived spread from the entryway to the back of the dining room. Curious faces turned to us in a movement that reminded me of a rock skipping across water; one group turned, then the next group noticed, until soon everyone was quiet and staring at us. Their eyes held silent questions. I was sure their mouths would unleash them as we drew near.

We scurried across the room, and grabbed a couple of stale cinnamon rolls that were about all that was left on the pastry table.

"Oh, shit!" I said. "Everyone is staring at us." Don't know why I expected it to be otherwise. "Shoot! 'Nosy Nora' is coming this way. Don't look." We quickly sat at the first empty table we could find.

Gert followed my lead, and we bowed our heads over the tired rolls on our plates. I pretended to say a prayer of thanks for our blessed old bread, which I never do and should have been a tip-off to Nora. But she backed off a bit. At least I had a few moments to think. My thoughts turned to the fact that Nora, being so inquisitive probably had a boatload of news on what people were saying. Maybe we could use her instead of playing her game. Nora enjoys spreading news as much as collecting it.

I ended my prayer, which had never begun, by saying, "Amen," and looked up.

"Good morning, Nora. Hasn't this been an awful morning?" I asked, shaking my head in disbelief.

"Oh, yes, especially for you two. What happened out there?"

"It was awful. What are people saying? Does anyone have a clue if Jake had any enemies?"

Nora made a quick shift to her news anchor persona and said, "Mabel and Eddie think it has something to do with a foreign person. You know he used to travel a lot. He knew lots of people in other countries through his business."

"Any specific countries?" I asked.

"They mentioned India and Japan. He was in the import business, you know."

"No," I said, wondering if I was wrong or they were. "Did they know the name of his business?"

"Eddie said they didn't know for sure. Thought it was "River" something. He thinks the last part had an "R" too, but he can't remember exactly."

By this time she had pulled an extra chair from a nearby table and plopped down between Gert and me.

Gertrude frowned and inched her chair a bit further away. I have mentioned her morals are a bit stricter than mine, haven't I? She finds gossip distasteful.

Shamelessly, pumping Nora for all I could get, I asked, "Have the police talked to you yet?"

"Yes, I was the first," she said, proudly. "I told them about the business connections. They were pleased to know that," she said, with an indulgent smile. "I also gave them information about Bonnie, his niece. I met her one time when she came to see Jake. A mousy little thing, I thought. Not at all like her uncle. He said she didn't come very often."

Nora, in her expensive red pant suit and sparkling earrings, felt most of us were mousy, and a little beneath her.

"I heard she lives here in town too," said Gert, to my surprise.

Maybe she'd had enough of Nora's 'know-it-all' attitude.

Nora gave Gert a "poor dear" hint of a smile and continued her diatribe. Clearly, she enjoyed her power position, and seemed to have lost sight of the fact that all information flowed from her mouth, not mine. Tsk, tsk.

"Yes," Nora continued. "I was told she lives in the historic-district of Walnut Street in one of those big old houses. Pretty, but expensive to keep up, I'd think. Does seem odd she didn't come more often, doesn't it?" Nora stood for a moment and appeared to be deep in thought. "Oh," she said, suddenly coming to life. "There's Mabel heading toward the basement. I'll ask her about Bonnie. I think she knew someone who knew her, a neighbor or something." She turned and disappeared into the crowd, leaving me to wonder what else we could have gotten out of her, but relieved she was gone,

The minute Nora left, others filled the space. We answered their questions as briefly as possible, mostly saying the police had told us not to talk about it, which they had.

We now stood encircled by people: like buzzards around roadkill.

"Let's get out of here," I whispered in Gert's ear. "This hasn't turned out as I'd hoped. Guess we need to let it rest for a bit. I'm tired of being stared at and pumped for information."

"Yeah," Gertrude agreed. "Let's go back to your place. There are too many people in here, and I can't bear to talk about it anymore. Some people are so thoughtless."

I could see tears starting to sparkle in her eyes again. I took her hand and led her past several people whose expression told me they would fire more questions if we didn't make a hasty exit. We hurried through the front door and headed down the walk. I was wondering just how close Gertrude and Jake had been. Maybe I'm just hard-nosed. I liked him too, but her pain seemed much deeper than mine. Was there more to the story?

"Joyce, did we leave your door open?" Gert asked, grabbing my arm.

From this distance, it was clear that my door was not completely closed.

"Hell, no! You know me. I don't water the plants on the porch without locking my door." We were now close enough to see the damage.

"Someone has jimmied my lock."

The door was open about six inches, and scratch marks were visible on the frame. I was afraid to go in. He, they, or whoever might still be inside. We backed off a short distance and ducked behind a lilac bush. I pulled out my cell and called the White Dove Retirement Center. I could see some police cars were still in the lot, along with a number of media vehicles.

When a voice answered, I said in my best, but poorly disguised voice, "This is the Springfield Police Department. Could I please speak to Detective Lancaster?"

"You certainly may. I'll get him for you," said our anxious-to-please receptionist.

I didn't want her to know it was me in case she got curious and peeked out the window. We didn't need anyone else in this dangerous situation.

Detective Lancaster and his partner were by our side within two minutes. We pointed at the door, and they took over. They drew their guns and motioned for us to stay back.

Gert and I retreated around the corner of Lucy Glenn's cottage, next door. I knew Lucy was in the dining room, so I wasn't worried about scaring the begeebers out of her. What was scary was one of us being hit by a stray bullet if gunshots erupted. Fortunately, the detective and his partner didn't take long to determine that the place was empty, at least of criminals. They came out, saw us peeking around Lucy's house, and motioned us over.

"Mrs. Greenly," said the detective, "We didn't find anyone, but can you come take a look and see if anything is missing? It appears they were looking for something. Pretty brazen breaking in the front door, but since your back door is visible to the parking lot, maybe they thought it was better than being seen by our people or the media."

Crossing the threshold, I felt violated. It seemed as if it was someone else's home. The place was a mess. It looked as if a rabid monkey had run through it. They had probably been in a big hurry. The culprit would have had no idea when I would come back, and the police were still on the premises. Who the hell would be brave enough or stupid enough to do this? I felt both chills and anger running through me as I gazed at the damage. My dresser looked like an ice cream cone in the Arizona sun. Bras, panties, and socks dripped over half open drawers. My jewelry box was dumped on a table. Various papers were pitched everywhere: old receipts, check registers, family snapshots. My bed covers had been thrown aside. It was obvious someone had looked under my mattress. In the kitchen, cabinet doors were open. I wanted to whip out the Clorox and scrub everything! Which is the equivalent of a near death experience for me. Damn-it-to-hell! I don't like people snooping in my space.

I took a quick look around, and didn't notice anything missing. Funny, how I didn't want to touch my own stuff. It seemed dirty and contaminated after some slime-ball had dug through everything, doing God knows what. The things were mine an hour ago, but now they seemed strange and toxic.

I had to pull myself together. There was one more thing that needed to be checked, but I'd wait until the police left. Wasn't sure how they'd feel about it.

"Can't see that anything is missing," I told Detective Lancaster.

"I'm going to have forensics come in and see if they can find some prints or anything else suspicious. Can you go to Mrs. Bush's cottage or back to the main building until we're finished?" he asked.

I glanced at Gert. She frowned and said, "Let's go to my place. I don't want to go back to that madhouse."

"Amen."

"If you discover something is gone after we leave, let me know. We'll be around here for a while. Also, I've been told you used to work for a PI and are pretty good at picking up on clues. If you see or hear anything that might help, please tell me. But, however tempting it may be, don't try to solve this on your own. Whoever did this is obviously very dangerous. We can't rule out it being someone here, but we have a long way to go before we can say who might be involved."

"By the way, have either of you ever seen anyone swimming in the lake?" he asked.

I looked at Gert standing just inside the door. Was she

wondering, as I was, if the police had found what we didn't have time to check out?

"No, can't say I have. Doesn't look like a good place, with the goose poop and all."

He nodded and said, "We'll have someone keep an eye on things around here tonight, so try not to worry. I don't know why someone would have done this, or what they were looking for, but since they've already looked, they shouldn't be back. Just try and relax. Get some rest. We'll let you know when our people are finished here."

"May I use my bathroom before we leave?"

"Go ahead. It doesn't look like it's been touched."

I scurried to the bath and closed the door. I didn't have to pee, but I wanted to check on something. I raised the lid on the toilet seat and tried to make believable sounds. Then I opened the door under the sink and dragged out a box of Depends I'd picked up at a garage sale for just this purpose. It felt heavy. Good!

I reached in and dug under a few layers. There it was! My old Glock 42. It was a compact little 380 cal., and had plenty of stopping power. I put it in the pocket of my jacket, covered it with a few tissues and a box of Gas-X. I left just enough sticking out so my now plump pocket looked like it held a few things I might need at Gert's, and not my old buddy from my days at the P.I. office. Jim and I both had our own guns after our scare.

It would be nice if I could change into something more suitable for hiding firearms, but that wasn't an option. I put the box back under the sink, flushed the stool, ran water for a bit, and left the bathroom.

Chapter 4

We walked out the front door and started over to Gert's place. She lives across the small lawn and two cottages east of me. Sidewalks intersect the lawn at intervals to make it easier for people to cross the grass.

"Gert," I said, "Let's walk down and take a look at the lake before we go to your place. I want to see if it's actually possible for someone to come in that way."

She nodded, knowing from long experience it was probably easier to go along than try to head me off.

We walked as far as the crime-scene tape, and gave the lake a good once-over.

"They sure couldn't come in from the north side," said Gert. "It's too shallow where the spring comes in, and the fence actually sits in the water."

"Yeah," I agreed. "And the woods are too far away. No one could climb a tree and swing over on a limb." Our observation passed swiftly over the gazebo. I hoped they would tear it down when this was over.

We turned our focus to the east fence that ran the length of the facility. The bank just inside the fence was covered in large rock; probably so there would be no grass to mow. It wasn't possible to get a mower across the water.

The south fence sat on a concrete dam made to form the

lake. In the middle, the fence was about two inches above the water for a distance of ten feet. This allowed water to flow over the dam and fall gracefully over large, carefully arranged rocks. It dropped about eight feet and cascaded into a small pool, which emptied into the city's storm drain. It's very pretty from the street and makes The White Dove look like an inviting place to live.

"Look. There are rocks and not just concrete where the water goes over. Do you suppose if someone climbed the waterfall, they could move some of the rocks around and have room to crawl under the fence?"

"Joyce, don't even consider that possibility! I can't stand the thought of someone getting in here without coming through the front door."

"Hold on to your britches. I'm not saying it's possible. Those rocks may not move at all. It's just a thought. If they can't be moved, I don't see how anyone could get in. The police will check it out, I'm sure."

I wasn't sure at all, but hoped it would make Gert relax. Besides, the police surely weren't that bad at their job.

"Right there is where Jim was standing," I said, pointing. Gert looked, but said nothing. She wasn't ready for the hunt.

We turned and walked in silence back to Gertrude's place. She unlocked the door and we went inside.

"What do you supposed they found at the lake?"

"Who knows," she answered, obviously not as interested as

I was.

"It must have been something that led them to believe a person could have swum under the fence."

Sitting down, my mind again went to the layout of the back lawn. How could the cop's theory work?

"Wonder what they could've found?" I said again, more to myself than to Gert.

"Joyce!" she said sharply. "Stop thinking about it. Did you not hear what the police said? We…namely you, are not to stick your nose in this mess."

"I didn't say I was going to do anything. Just thinking. They did say if we thought of anything, to let them know. If we don't think, then how can we be good citizens and help our law-enforcement." It was difficult to make my inquisitive urges sound noble, so she wouldn't ruin my investigation. Oh, yes. There would be one! I could no more let this go than bypass a glass of sweet tea in the Sahara.

"Okay, but let's just stick to thinking."

With the gate now partially open, I said, "What shape do you think the thing we saw at the lake was?"

"Maybe sort of oval. It looked black; a dark color, at least."

"That's what I saw too. It wasn't shiny like metal; if it was metal, it had a dull finish. Agreed?"

"Well," Gert said thoughtfully, "I don't know for sure. Couldn't see it clearly at that distance, but it didn't look shiny to me either."

"If they're asking us about someone swimming in the lake, it must have been something that would suggest that."

For a few minutes we sat in silence. Gert's place was so clean and organized; it was a little difficult to get my thoughts together. My place is not dirty, but I work better in a bit of clutter.

"Swimming trunks?" Gertrude offered.

"Probably not. He would have had to walk off naked. Could have had clothes in a waterproof bag, but that would've made it tough to swim and get under the fence. Guess he could have thrown a bag over and onto the lawn. This is assuming he could fit under it himself. That seems like a hell of a lot of trouble. Besides, where's the damn bag? What we saw was not that large."

"Goggles?" she suggested next.

"Bingo. That would be about right for the shape and size."

"Not to change the subject, but I'm going to fix some tea," said Gert. "You want me to make you some coffee? I know you're not much of a tea person."

"No, tea is fine for me, too."

"I have some Fig Newtons, if you'd like some. It's almost lunchtime. I'd rather not go to the dining room, but I am a little hungry."

"Sure, cookies sound good."

"In fact," Gertrude yelled from the kitchen, "Why don't we go to Red Lobster for dinner tonight. I don't think I can stand being around the residents here anymore today."

"That's a great idea," I replied, quite pleased. Getting a good look at the waterfall from the outside was at the top of my list, and this would be a perfect excuse to see it from the street.

We sat quietly, eating cookies and drinking tea for probably an hour. I don't know what was going through my best friend's head, but mine was filled with How-To questions: how to get Jake's personal information: how to find out what the police found in the water: how to find our killer.

There was a knock on the door. We jumped like spooked rabbits. Gert recovered, and opened the door to another law-enforcement officer.

"Are you Mrs. Greenly?" he asked.

"No, but she's here," Gert replied.

By this time I was standing beside her.

"What is it? I'm Mrs. Greenly."

"Detective Lancaster wanted me to let you know we're finished with your place. You can go back, if you want."

"Thank you." I did want to go back to my place, and I'm sure Gert had had enough of me, and my probing questions.

"Do you want me to come help you clean up?" Gert asked, as the officer walked away.

"No, no that's fine." "You get some rest. I'll come get you around 4:30. I'll drive."

Gertrude nodded her head in approval, and closed the door.

31

We were both numb and dimwitted at this point. I felt like a sleepwalker on autopilot. I wanted to go home, but, hell, I have to admit, it didn't seem as welcoming as it had this morning.

As I approached, I could see a guy from Gold's Locks, installing a new lock on my door.

"Hi" he said. "I'll be finished here in a minute. I'm putting some wood filler in the gouges around the facing and in the door. We'll let it dry tonight. Mr. Bennett said he would have your handyman touchup the paint tomorrow."

"Appreciate you getting on it so fast."

"No problem. Here are your new keys. I rekeyed the back door, so they would be the same," he replied.

"Thanks." I took them and scooted past him into my place. Within seconds the bed was stripped down to the bare mattress. I gathered the sheets, pillowcases, etc., in a big ball and stuffed them in a laundry bag. Sleeping on any part of them was not an option. There were plenty of clean sheets in the linen closet, but no extra mattress cover. We could run by Walmart and get a new one while we were out tonight.

I grabbed a can of Lysol from under the bathroom sink, and started spraying. Don't know if it's possible to O.D. on Lysol fumes, but it was a little overwhelming. I soon had to stand outside for a bit, with the windows and doors open. The man had finished with my front door and was gone, so there was no explanation needed for my hasty exit. Damn, I had things to do other than stand on the porch gasping for air.

When I could breathe again, every surface was sprayed with disgust and pissed-off fury. If I had any idea who did this, I'd use more than sanitizing spray on them! Opening the cabinet doors in the kitchen, everything that was possible to spray without poisoning myself was soon glistening with disinfectant.

After that, another trip outside was needed. I was getting lightheaded again. Damn-it-to-hell. It must have been Jake's killer who did this. What was he looking for? Coming through the door, my eyes fell on the jewelry that had been dumped on the coffee table. A light bulb popped on in my head. Was he, they, or whoever, thinking I had the stickpin? The police hadn't given any information about what they'd found, except to Gert and me. And that was only so they could determine if it belonged to Jake. It must be important to the killer. Damn! What was there about it that would make a murderer do such a stupid thing to try and get it back? This was just a theory, of course, but I couldn't imagine anything else that would cause someone to take such a risk. They could have been caught, and it would have been all over for them; or me too, if I'd walked in and found them pointing a gun at me! Hells bells! Don't want to think about that scenario!

"Mr. Bennett asked me to come see if you needed any help."

The voice was Big Jim Landis. I stumbled and fell on one

knee. How in hell could someone his size move so quietly?

Before I could answer, he grabbed my arm and said, "Didn't mean to scare you. Just trying to help. You okay?"

No, I wasn't okay. I'd skinned my knee, but I said, "I'm fine. I'm fine. Just didn't hear you walk up. I don't need any help. Thank you anyway." I wanted to say, 'Now, get the hell off my porch,' but I kept it to myself.

"Okay, let me know if you need something," he said, as he turned and lumbered away as quietly as he arrived.

Had Bennett sent him? I was a ball of nerves. Maybe he was totally innocent, but the picture of him staring through the fence hung in my head like a bad dream.

Back inside, I finished putting things away. A few items were still damp from my spraying crusade; had to spread them on the counter to finish drying. A look at the clock said it was time to get cleaned up for dinner.

I took a quick shower, dressed and hurried over to Gert's. Being late is right up there with lying in my book. One of my pet peeves is when people don't respect others enough to keep their promise of a time agreed upon. Panting a bit, I rang her doorbell at exactly 4:30.

She came to the door, and proud of myself for making it on time, I was expecting maybe a smile and a few kind words. That's not at all what happened.

"Joyce, why in the world can't you dress like everyone else? I've told you a dozen times; those frilly anklets should not to be worn with heels. And, we know you like to wear mismatched earrings, but those just don't work at all. Neither one of them goes with the dress you're wearing."

"Well, good evening to you, too! You know how I am. I refuse to be a damn toothpick lost in a box of a hundred others. Being different is enjoyable." To me I looked just fine. "Are you saying you don't want to be seen with me?"

"Oh, no," said Gert, squirming a bit. "I'm so sorry. I understand you have your own style. It just seems you went a little off track this evening."

I walked over and looked at myself in her mirror. "Maybe at bit." I said, actually thinking I looked damn good. "Could have been the Lysol fumes," I said, trying to appease her.

"Oh, you're my best friend in the world," Gert offered. "This has been a nightmare of a day! I should have kept my big mouth shut. Please forgive me. Let's just go have a nice dinner and try to get back to normal. If that's possible."

If there was one thing Gert didn't have it was a big mouth. It was amazing she'd said something negative at all. "Don't worry about it," I replied. "You're right. This has been a horrendous day. Neither of us are our normal selves right now. Let's go relax."

I could have made a catty little remark about how prim and properly Gert was dressed (boring), but figured this wasn't the time, and besides, it would violate my 'You be you, and I'll be me' policy.

"Remind me to stop at Walmart on the way home. I need a new mattress cover."

"Will do," Gert agreed.

We walked through the main building, signed out and went to my car. It's a bright red Corvette, something I always wanted, and my late husband would never allow. God bless his soul; he never really understood me. He tolerated things many men would not have, but the car was just too much. Of course, I would have gotten it anyway, if I'd really wanted to, but he was good to me. I'm aware of my tendency to be a bit difficult once in a while, so I just kept it on my bucket list while he was alive. But hot damn, I love it now!

It's a bit extravagant, but I'm a lot like my grandmother. She pinched pennies on a lot of things, but if she 'really' wanted something, she bought the best: to hell with the price. Maybe I inherited that little trait.

We climbed in and turned down the road that went by the waterfall. I drove slowly, taking a careful look. It was hard to see exactly what the rocks were like on top, but with so much water running over them, it seemed they would surely move or wiggle a bit if they weren't cemented together. Also, it would take a mountain goat, or someone way younger than seventy-two to climb the hell up there.

"Why are you going so slow?" Gert asked, breaking my train of thought.

"Just thinking."

"You had better not be thinking about doing what the police told us 'not' to do. You know what they said."

"Sorry, I'm kind of tired," I waffled. Gert needed some down time, unlike me. I thrive on catching bad guys or bad girls. Yes, there have always been bad women, but years ago, especially in the South, people didn't want to believe it was possible. After all, we are so delicate and helpless. What a crock.

I sure wasn't marking any females off my list of killers in regard to Jake's murder. It did seem, however, it would have been difficult for a woman to overpower him and drag his body to the gazebo. She might have had a partner though. There were all sorts of combinations: one man, two men, one man and one woman, or even two women. A lot to think about! "Let it rest," I told myself, as I turned into Red Lobster.

We enjoyed our meal immensely. We each took down more than our share of those heavenly little cheesy biscuits. Damn, those things are addictive. We both ate a lobster, shrimp combo, and had just begun to push our lousy day into the background, when I looked up and spotted Eddie and Mabel. They were walking near the front of the room speaking with a hostess. Eddie was pointing toward a door to a room north of us, and they disappeared around the corner. I was sure they didn't see us, and Gert had her back to them. My mind tried to decide if I should mention it or not. One look at Gertrude's face and 'not' won out. She appeared relaxed for the first time today. This information could wait until tomorrow, but what the hell? I didn't think Mabel and Eddie even liked each other. Tolerated each other would be a better description of their relationship, as I saw it. They never shared a table at The White Dove: never walked together: spoke very little. Had I missed something?

"Joyce?"

"Sorry, Gert. I'm a bit off tonight. Did you say something?"

"Well, I can certainly understand that. I just said, I'm finished, if you are. Why don't we go get your mattress cover, and we can both get settled for the evening?"

"Works for me." Besides, I thought to myself, I would rather not run into Eddie or Mabel if one of them decided to take a trip to the bathrooms that were located in the front lobby. For some reason, I felt it was better if they didn't know I'd seen them.

We made the stop at Walmart, got the mattress cover, and headed home. I tried to take another look at the waterfall, but there were lights at the top and more near the bottom that pretty much blinded me from seeing any meaningful detail.

I parked, we signed in and headed down the sidewalk toward our cottages.

"Goodnight, Joyce," said Gert, with a gentle squeeze to my arm. "Hope you sleep well."

"The same to you. I'll come get you for breakfast in the morning,"

Chapter 5

My new key worked just fine. I hadn't even closed the door
yet, and was throwing my Walmart sack on the sofa when I
heard, "JOYCE!"

I recognized Gert's terrified, booming yell. It scared the
pants off me! I swear to hell, I don't know how her small body
can produce that kind of volume.

"What on earth?" I yelled, running as fast as my skinned
knee would allow.

A few people poked their heads out their doors and looked
in our direction. Most were in their nightclothes, or they might
have ventured further.

As I arrived at her door, she was standing on the porch with
tears streaming down her face. Silently she pulled the door
back and showed me a room almost identical to the one at my
place this morning. Bed turned inside out, drawers open and
spilling on the floor, and cabinets open with the contents
littering the counters. If anything, Gert's looked worse than
mine. Maybe they felt they had more time.

"Holy hell! Has the world gone mad?" I hugged my friend
and said, "It will be all right, Gert. We'll get through this."

I called 911 for the second time that day. While we waited,
we looked around the room. This time the intruders had come
through the rear door. Gert's place backs up to another row of

cottages that face away from her, a much safer set-up for thieves. Besides, he, they or whoever, had removed the light bulb near the back door. Damn, sleazy scum.

"You may as well use this time to see if anything is missing, Gert. Maybe we won't have to stick around so long after the cops get here."

In a fog, Gert walked from one mess to another and looked without touching. I'm not sure it would matter if she handled things or not. They hadn't found a single print or even a smudge at my place.

We heard sirens in the distance. A few minutes later the police and Mr. Bennett arrived at the door. Now every cottage had a face or two sticking out the door, and the night workers were lined up at the door of the White Dove. They resembled buzzards on a limb staring at a dying chicken. I could almost hear, "What in the hell have those two done now?" floating in the night air.

We explained to the officer in charge what had happened, and this time Gert managed to speak coherently.

"I will let Detective Lancaster know the situation," said the officer. "You say nothing is missing that you know of?"

Gert nodded.

"I'm afraid I'll have to ask you to leave while we have someone process the scene. Do you have somewhere you can go until we're finished?" he asked.

Mr. Bennett stepped up to us and said, "I'm so sorry this

has happened to both of you. I feel responsible. I'll have our night manager call University Plaza, and the White Dove will put you up for the night. It's the least we can do."

"That's awfully nice of you," I said. "We'll take you up on it, won't we, Gert?"

She gave a weak nod of approval.

He stepped outside and used the walkie on his wrist to call the front desk.

"Can I get a robe, nightgown and a change of clothes?" Gert asked the officer.

"Sure. Take these gloves, so you won't disturb any evidence. I doubt, however, clothing was their target."

We made a quick stop at my place so I could grab a few things we felt hadn't been touched, and headed to my car. The night manager of The White Dove told us our reservations were made and gave us a sad smile as we passed through the lobby. Damn, what a ghastly, terrible day! I wanted to get as far from this place as possible: as fast as possible. We didn't say a word to each other until we pulled into the parking lot at the hotel.

A very nice clerk checked us in and pointed us to our room on the fourth floor. We were given a single room with two queen size beds. It was very cozy and thankfully, nothing in it reminded us in the least of home. We were soon in our pajamas and under the covers. I have to admit, even for me, it was nice to have Gert in the room. It was much better than being alone after what we'd been through. My head was twirling with the day's events, and I could hear Gert tossing around in the other bed. How is it possible to turn off the murder of one of your best friends, and two damn home invasions in one day? It was too much.

Gert seemed to drop off around two, and I think it was somewhere around three for me. We both slept a little past our usual five-thirty, but it was still a short night. Coming to life, I had a few seconds of unspoiled peace, before the previous day smacked me in the face. Hell fire! I wanted to retreat, but the warm-fuzzy was viciously yanked from me.

I saw my roommate stirring.

"Gert, want me to fix you a cup of coffee? Maybe we can watch the news before we get breakfast?"

"Sure," she answered softly. "I hope you slept better than I did."

"Afraid not. Don't feel much better than when I went to bed. Think it's going to take a day or two," I said, as I ran water in the little coffee pot. "Oh, I forgot to tell you something. Last night when we were eating, I saw Eddie and Mabel come in together. They were seated in another room near the front door. Did you know they were friends?"

"No. I don't remember ever seeing them speak to each other. Eddie usually sits with his buddies and Mabel spends time with Grace and Nora for the most part. I don't guess it's any of our business what they do though."

As I said earlier, Gertrude has very little tolerance for gossip. I was on my own with this little puzzle.

I dropped the subject and turned on the morning news. Crap! Should have known better. First thing up was a big story about Jake's murder. We were shocked to see our own faces plastered across the screen. Damn reporters must have taken them with a high-powered lens. We hadn't seen them at all. I grabbed the remote and flipped to a cooking channel that I'm sure neither of us focused on. Gert headed for the bathroom. We took turns using the shower and changing into clean clothes. When not in the bathroom, each of us sat staring at the TV, seeing nothing. I can't say if they were making a soufflé or roasting a damn goat.

When we were both clean, and dressed, we left the room like zombies and took the glass elevator to the main floor. At the back of the room we found a generous breakfast bar. I don't know about Gert, but food was not a high priority at the moment. I spooned gravy over a biscuit, got a cup of coffee, and sat at the most private table I could find. Gert was right behind me.

As she sat down she said, "Joyce, I'm going to call Janet and see if she can stay with me for a couple of days. This is a lot to deal with. I need some family with me. I should have called her last night? I hope it wasn't on the news in Kansas City."

"It surely wasn't, or at least she didn't see it," I reassured her. "She would have called you already."

"Do you think I'm being a big baby?" she said, with tears beginning to glisten.

"Of course not," I answered, but was thinking I sure as hell didn't want either of my boys here. They would shut down my investigation if it meant putting their mother in a straightjacket! It would be nice to see them, of course, but this wasn't the time. Gert's case was different.

"Do you think Janet will be able to get off work?"

"She shouldn't have a problem. She and Roger seldom use their vacation days since Katie and Brian are getting older. They are so involved in sports and their friends; they don't really want to take a trip with mom and dad. You know how kids are now."

"Yes, it's different than it used to be," I said, not really knowing first hand. My sons haven't come up with even one child between them. I do, however, see children when I'm out shopping. Some of them say things to their parents that would have gotten me several whacks with a peach tree switch.

We left our plates with less than half the food eaten.

Chapter 6

Our drive to the White Dove produced no joyful thoughts of returning to our once peaceful homes. Gert had called Janet from the hotel and she was now anxious to clean her place before her daughter arrived. She declined my offer to help. It was clear she wanted some time to herself. Couldn't blame her. So did I: time to find some damn clues. That had to be done on my own.

First on my list was Bonnie, Jake's niece. Mabel might be able to help. At least Nora thought she knew where she lived. First, it was necessary to look at the list of resident cottage numbers. Most of my encounters with Mabel were in the dining area. I wanted to be sure I had the right place before knocking on doors.

The front lobby was empty except for a clerk on the phone. It didn't take long to see Mabel lived in cottage thirty-three. Fannie and a couple more employees could be seen through a glass wall several feet behind the front desk. If Mabel couldn't help me, I hoped Fannie would let me peek at Jake's file.

I walked down the sidewalk, and knocked on Mabel's front door. No answer. I tried again. Nothing. Damn it to hell! It's a bitch to be in P.I. mode and have to stifle it. Where was she? Cool it, Joyce, I told myself. She could be a lot of places: visiting someone, doing laundry, or reading a book in the library. She was on the grounds somewhere, or at least she hadn't signed out. I'd looked when we checked in.

My tummy growled to remind me most of my breakfast had been left on the plate. Maybe a glass of tea and a couple of cookies would be a pleasant distraction, and help me think more clearly. If Mabel was out and about, I might even see her. Retracing my steps to the lobby, I entered the cozy little snack room. My butt had hardly touched the chair when Mabel and Nadine, a new resident I had seen but not met, came into the room.

"Hi, Joyce," said Mabel.

"Hello there, Mabel. Would you two like to join me? I haven't officially met Nadine yet."

"Sure. We'll get our drinks and be right over," answered Mabel, turning her short, slightly plump body toward the beverage counter. Age had not been kind to Mabel. It was apparent she had once been an attractive woman, but the extra pounds had landed in unflattering places. She was, however, always dressed nicely.

They soon returned and we settled like old friends around a small table with comfy chairs. Mabel introduced us to each other.

"Nice to meet you, Nadine. Are you from around here?"

"Jefferson City actually, but my son and his family live near Springfield, so I moved to be closer to them."

"Mornin', ladies."

We looked up to see Eddie poking his head around the door, a big silly grin across his face. Mabel's smile was pretty dim, and I'm not sure I gave him a very inviting look either.

He took the hint. "Well, see you later. Got things to do," he said disappearing around the doorframe.

"He's not one of my favorites," Mabel whispered to Nadine. "You may like him though. Don't listen to me."

Shit! The perfect opportunity, and I couldn't say anything with Nadine here.

A scream reverberated through the morning air; mixed with thumps and bangs. A male scream is the worst kind. When a man screams, it is not because of a mouse. It's usually serious. This was one of the bad ones.

Our hearts beat like rabbits under a diving eagle. We were paralyzed for a few seconds.

"What the hell?" I said, leaping to my feet. As I ran to the hallway, I looked back and saw Mabel and Nadine close behind. The hall was empty. We hurried to the basement stairs from where the sounds had come. We were met with a horrifying sight. Eddie was lying crumpled and bleeding at the bottom. His limbs were contorted in unnatural angles.

I carefully inched my way toward him, clinging to the bannister for moral and physical support. Eddie's body had fallen to one side, which left room for me to step carefully past his twisted body. He seemed to be trying to speak, so I knelt on the floor near his head.

"Pu-pu-shed," he whispered, his mouth bleeding and his eyes closed.

Mr. Bennett appeared from nowhere and hurried past Mabel and Nadine who were cowering at the top of the stairs.

"Is he alive?" he asked, looking at me.

"I'm pretty sure he is," I answered, feeling Eddie's wrist for a pulse. It was weak, but it was there.

"Did you see him fall?" Mr. Bennett asked, looking at me, and then up at the two visibly shaken women.

"No, we were in the snack room," I answered. "We heard his scream and ran to see what happened."

"Call 911," he said, pushing the button on his wrist. "We need an ambulance," he shouted. "He must have tripped or something. I think he comes down to play pool quite often, or he might have been doing his laundry," offered Mr. Bennett. "Terrible accident."

I glanced around the basement; relieved to see Gert hadn't made it here with her laundry yet. I had to head her off. She didn't need to see this.

"Excuse me a minute, if you will," I said to Mr. Bennett. "I need to warn a friend not to come here until the ambulance has taken Eddie to the hospital."

"Sure, we need to stop anyone from coming in here." He stood up, locked the door and used his walkie to request a "Closed" sign.

I called Gert and told her the basement was closed for some

reason, so to hold her laundry until tomorrow. Thankfully, she didn't ask any questions.

"You ladies can go, if you like. I'll stay until the ambulance arrives," said Mr. Bennett.

"I think I will stay, if you don't mind. Mabel and Nadine can go if they want," I said.

Mr. Bennett gave me a very unenthusiastic hint of a smile. Nadine and Mabel scooted off; they looked relieved. Not me! I felt like a guard dog. Eddie's attempt at speaking had sounded suspiciously like "pushed." Had someone deliberately pushed him down the stairs? If so, who and why? I wasn't leaving until he was headed for the hospital. The basement was a walkout. They would probably have to bring the stretcher around the building, and to the door that was now locked. Besides, I also wanted to find out which hospital they were taking him to. Once again, we heard sirens nearing the White Dove.

"I had better go tell them to come around to this door," said Mr. Bennett as he started up the stairs. Mabel and Nadine were nowhere to be seen.

I was left with Eddie, wondering if I had heard his last word, and if he really had said 'pushed'. If so, why would someone want to do that? Who was Eddie? I really didn't know anything about him. Did anyone else?

A few minutes later, I heard a key in the outside lock. Mr. Bennett opened the door for the emergency crew. I stood up, and moved out of the way.

"Is he alive?" Mr. Bennett asked the medics as they examined him.

"Yes," answered the one holding Eddie's hand. "We'll take good care of him," he said looking at Mr. Bennett, and seeming to notice me for the first time. "Are you a relative?" he asked.

"No, just a friend," I said, stretching the truth. "Can you tell me if he's going to Cox or Mercy?" I asked.

"He's going to Mercy," he answered, as he hurried to get Eddie secured.

"Thanks, I appreciate it," which I did. Now I'd know where to call and find out when they would allow visitors. It was important to connect any dots surrounding the White Dove and Jake, and there were a lot of dots. He must have known Eddie to some extent, if Eddie knew what Jake had done for a living. And Mabel? How did she know…maybe Eddie told her? Too many loose ends.

It was not pleasant watching the medics put Eddie on the stretcher. It was apparent at least one arm and one leg must be broken. They worked to move his injured limbs into more realistic positions. His head and mouth were bloody. Even if he wasn't a friend, so to speak, even "tough old me" had to feel sorry for the guy. I wanted him to be okay just because he was a human, and also because I desperately wanted to ask him some questions. Did someone push him, if so, who and why? Where did they go?

Should I tell Detective Lancaster what I thought Eddie had said? But, he had indicated they thought it was someone from outside that had killed Jake…or did he just say that to throw me off? Would he put a guard outside Eddie's door if I told him? Did he need someone outside his door? Oh, hell! This was complicated. I just wanted to be his first visitor…if he made it.

Following the stretcher out the door, I headed for Gertrude's place. I wanted to tell her what happened before someone else did. She was sorting things in stacks to replace them in the proper drawers; if she felt they were not too contaminated. After a brief and less graphic version of Eddie falling down the stairs, I told her the laundry room was now available. Gert always did her own laundry. I pay extra to have mine done. I'm not lazy. I just don't like domestic chores, as I said before.

Next, was cottage thirty-three. Surely, Eddie's fall had ended the hospitality tour Mabel had been giving Nadine. Knock. Knock. I heard shuffling inside. Hallelujah! Someone was home.

The door opened. Oh, damn-it-to-hell! It was Nadine.

"Oh, Joyce," she said. "I was just on my way out. I want to call my son and tell him what happened. It was so horrible," she exclaimed, lips quivering and eyes glistening with tears.

Damn! I must be stranger than I thought. Everyone but me

seems to gather their kids around when they have a scare. What the hell, I thought. My method may be different, but it works for me. My sons would be packing my things and updating my passport, or at least they'd try. I'd win in the end, but who wants the hassle.

"I'm so sorry we didn't get to visit, Nadine," I said, trying to put my best foot forward. "Maybe we can do better next time."

"Yes, I hope so," she said, and scurried down the sidewalk.

Relieved she was gone; I turned to Mabel, who was now standing in the doorway.

"What happened after we left?" she asked. "Is he going to be alright?"

"The ambulance took him to the hospital. He was alive, but I'm sure it will take some time for the doctors to determine how seriously he's injured."

"I feel so bad saying what I did about not caring for Eddie," Mabel exclaimed. "It will haunt me forever."

"Don't feel bad. We all say things we wish we could take back. It was just unfortunate timing. You had no idea what was about to happen. Was he rude to you or something? Is that why you don't care for him?"

"No, not exactly," Mabel answered. "He just seemed to always be asking questions about people."

"Like who?" I asked, hoping to get the answer I was digging for.

Mabel paused and looked down at her shoes for a few seconds, as if they could give her some advice on what to say.

"Oh, I don't know," she said, looking up at me. "Well, Jake's niece, Bonnie, for one. I know very little about her, but he just kept bugging me. A friend of mine lives next door to her on Walnut St. She doesn't know her well either. They just speak occasionally if they run into each other on the sidewalk. I don't think Bonnie is out and about a lot."

Mabel hesitated, and stared into space for a few seconds. "That's all I know, but Eddie wouldn't leave me alone about her, and Jake. I made the mistake of letting him talk me into to going to dinner with him last night. I love to eat out, but it turned into another question and answer marathon, and I was very agitated by the time I got back," she said, pulling at her skirt.

I didn't mention that I knew about the dinner.

"Where are my manners?" Mabel exclaimed, backing away from the door. "Come in and have a seat."

Holy shit! Oh God, I almost said that out loud. Entering the room, I was bombarded with wall-to-wall doilies, embroidered wall hangings, pillow covers and lacey mats on every table, sofa and chair! The woman's life must consist of nothing but handiwork. A basket of thread adorned with a variety of crochet hooks sat on the floor near an overstuffed chair. Lord, I needed air. All this domesticity was suffocating me. I looked for the least lacy spot and carefully perched on the edge of a chair, trying to act as normal as possible. Handiwork is like spiders to me. I can take a few, but it seemed there were hundreds. My mind spun a picture of the pieces flying through the air and wrapping around my face in an attempt to mummify me.

Praise of her work was in order, but I couldn't bring myself to mention it. What could have happened in my childhood to cause this idiotic reaction? This is your problem, Joyce, not hers. P.I. work can be a bitch sometimes, especially when surrounded by lace. I took a deep breath and continued.

"I'm sorry. The last twenty four hours haven't been very pleasant for you have they?" Attempting to sound sympathetic, I was feeling very guilty knowing my mission was the same as Eddie's. I moved my hand, trying to avoid touching an offensive piece and clasped my fingers together in my lap.

"Oh, I'm okay," Mabel, answered. "I just feel bad about him getting hurt right after I said something ugly about him."

"Why do you suppose he thought you knew anything about Jake and Bonnie?"

"I'm not sure, but I suspect maybe Nora made him think I did. I don't want to say anything bad about anyone else though. I've learned my lesson after what just happened." she murmured, giving her shoes another look. She seemed to be shrinking into a pitiful ball of guilt.

"You may be right about this one though," I told her, trying to lighten the mood. "Nora did tell Gert and me that you knew something about Bonnie and about Jake's job, before he retired."

"Oh, gracious!" she exclaimed, putting a hand over her mouth. "I should know better than to say things around her."

"I don't believe half of what she says," I offered. "She just can't help herself. Did you know Jake very well? I can't believe he's gone."

"Not really. He was always such a nice, polite man, but I didn't visit with him much. In fact, I think what I knew about his job, came from overhearing a conversation when Eddie was talking to some people. Somehow he got the idea I knew more. There seems to be a lot of misinformation going around. I'm amazed he wasn't trying to ask you and Gertrude about him."

"We didn't stay here last night and haven't been to the main building much. I wonder why he wants to know about Jake and Bonnie. Maybe he's like Nora, just full of curiosity."

I didn't think that at all. I felt there was something else going on, but I needed more information. It was difficult to keep my mind on the task at hand, and off the dreadful threads surrounding me.

Oh, shit! A casual glance toward the basket near Mabel's chair, and I nearly peed my pants. A gun butt was peeking between the hateful balls of thread! My heart thumped and my mind was like a frenzied hamster on a wheel. I forced my eyes back to Mabel and tried to calm myself.

"Mabel, I do hate to bring up Bonnie, after what you've already been through, but Gert and I would like to send a card, some flowers, or do s-s-something. Would your neighbor mind giving us her address? I guess we need her last name too, if she has it. I don't know if it is the same as Jake's or something d-different."

Oh, damn! I sound like Gert. Hold it together, Joyce. A gun and threads! What does the gun mean, and the threads were destroying my ability to summon up reasonable thoughts.

"I don't think she would mind at all. You two were such good friends with Jake. I'm so sorry. I understand why you would want to pay your respects. I'll call her and get back to you. I could've done it for Eddie too, but I felt he was being nosy."

"Thanks so much. We really appreciate it." At least I did; Gert didn't have a clue.

Hell, I have to get out of here, now. I wanted a better look at the basket, but there was no way to take a peek without Mabel seeing me.

"I'm going to get out of your hair for now. I'll talk to you later if you get Bonnie's information." I forced myself to walk to the door like a sane person. We said goodbye, and I left confused and wondering who the hell I'd been talking with.

Chapter 7

I had taken only a few steps when my cell phone rang, and scared the tar out of me. I was still half witted, and spooked.

"Hello?"

"This is Detective Lancaster. I hear you were at the scene when Eddie Thompson fell down the basement stairs. I'm in the main building. I'd like to ask you a few questions. Do you want me to come to your cottage or would you rather meet me in the office?"

"I'd prefer my place, if you don't mind." I felt better knowing no one could hear what I had to say, just in case.

"Okay. I'll see you in a few minutes," he said, and I heard a click on his end.

On the way to my place, I scrolled through my phone to give Gert a call. I needed to fill her in on what I'd said to Mabel. Had to cover my tracks in case Mabel ran into Gert first. The part about wanting to do these things was not a lie. I'm sure Gert would want to send her condolences as I did, but I also wanted more information about Jake.

I looked up just in time to see Gertrude and her daughter, Janet, coming out of the main building. They were too far away for me to yell, so I hit Gert's number in 'My Favorites'. With the detective coming, I didn't have time to walk over to them. They spotted me and gave big waves.

Gert picked up, and I quickly filled her in on what happened at Mabel's, except for the gun and threads part. We hung up, and waved again. Janet had her arm around her mother, which is what I'm sure Gert needed most. What I needed was my buddy, Gert, so I could bounce ideas off her. Even if she wasn't always a willing participant, she was a good listener. Right now, however, she needed some time to relax with her daughter. I was on my own.

I glanced toward my place, and realized the western sky had darkened. It looked as if a pretty strong storm was headed our way. I hadn't seen the weather report since before Jake was killed. The world was going on even if some of us were not tuned in.

A big gust of wind hit me as I reached the porch. Det. Lancaster was visible as he left the main building. He had tucked a raincoat under his arm. I rushed inside to make some coffee.

The sound of the doorbell and hail pelting the roof arrived together. I hurried to let the detective inside. The porch was not large enough to offer much protection.

"Come in. Boy, that came up fast, didn't it," I said, ushering him into the room and closing the door behind him.

"Sure did. It's nasty out there. How are you? I hear you've been in the wrong place at the wrong time again."

"You're right about that," I admitted, smiling grimly. "Would you like some coffee or tea before we start? I'm sure you have lots of questions."

"Coffee would be great. Just black, thanks," he answered, sitting square in my favorite chair.

Damn, what is it with that chair! You'd think you could sit where you want in your own house. Should have put my purse there instead of on the table, I grumbled to myself.

Two cups in hand, I served one to Det. Lancaster and took mine to my second favorite chair.

"What do you want to know?" I asked.

"I understand you, Mabel and a new tenant, Nadine, were in the snack room when Eddie fell down the steps. Can you tell me what happened?"

Wind, rain, and thunder made it necessary to talk louder than I would have liked. I went through the story, including Mabel's dislike for Eddie, and even though it hurt like hell, I told him what Eddie had said to me. Damn, I hated to, but I hoped it would inspire him to put a guard with Eddie. I really needed to ask him some questions. It wouldn't be good to have someone finish him off before one of us got some answers. I prayed he was going to recover enough for that to be possible.

The only part this informant left out was the gun in Mabel's crochet basket. Maybe she was like me and felt she needed it for protection, or maybe she was a 'bad girl'. I wanted to keep it to myself until I knew which. Somehow guns and lace didn't seem right.

"So you really think he said, 'Pushed'?"

"I'm pretty sure he did. You're the only one I've told. It's hard to tell who can be trusted."

"Your P.I. experience coming through?" he said, with a slight twinkle in his eyes.

"Maybe, but you know what they say about 'loose lips'. I just felt it might be important, with everything else going on around here. What if someone was trying to kill him?"

"You were right to keep it to yourself, and just in case he's in danger, I'm going to have a guard posted outside his door. If he makes it, he might have something to tell us about Jake's murder."

Hallelujah, just what I wanted to hear.

"Do you suppose I could be put on the visitor's list?" I asked, my heart beating like a runner at the finish line. It would be hard to sneak in, but I'd try if necessary.

"I think that could be arranged. He might tell you things he wouldn't say to us, but you have to promise to tell me everything he says; no holding back," he said, looking me square in the eyes with his brows furrowed. "We'll have to see if or when he's able. Also, you realize talking to him could put you in more danger, if someone actually did try to kill him," he said, as if he'd just processed that scenario.

"This isn't my first rodeo, you know," I said, trying to look calmer than I felt. Maybe I should tell him about my Concealed Carry permit, but what the hell, he might already know. I'm sure they'd been checking everyone's background.

Damn! I'd just keep that little tidbit to myself; in case he didn't know and it might turn into a problem. What I was going to do, was get my Glock 42 back out of the Depends box and put it in my purse where I could get my hands on it.

"Yes, I know about your past experience," said Det. Lancaster, setting his cup down and giving me a stern look. "You need to let the police take care of this. I know your tenacious personality makes it hard to sit back and watch, but you could put us in a worse situation if we have to worry about protecting you as well."

"I understand your concern," I said, trying to sound reasonable. "But it seems to me no one in this facility is safe. If someone did push Eddie down the stairs, who's to say there might not be more people on the hit list? I swear to you I will be careful, but I will be on the look-out for any clues that might help find the killer or killers," I said, looking the detective in the eyes. Hot damn! I sounded a lot tougher than I felt.

"Well, I guess we know where we stand," Det. Lancaster said, with a look of resignation on his face. "Just be careful. I don't want to see anything happen to you, or Gertrude. I'll talk to the other two ladies and hope they're not as feisty as you," he said, with the hint of a smile.

He stood, put on his raincoat and walked to the door. The wind and hail had passed, but it was still pouring outside. He nodded, pulled a hood over his head, and made a run toward

Mabel's place.

As I closed the door, it dawned on me; I hadn't eaten since early this morning. I glanced at the clock and was surprised to see it was almost three p.m. I wasn't thrilled at the prospect of running through the rain to find food, so I rummaged around and found a loaf of bread in the fridge and a jar of peanut butter in the cabinet. This was pretty much my only choice since I'd cleaned out and soaked almost everything with Lysol after the break-in. I definitely needed a trip to the grocery store, but for now, I made a peanut butter sandwich and poured myself another cup of coffee.

Chapter 8

RING! Oh hell! I almost fell on the floor trying to reach my phone. I must have fallen asleep in my chair, and so had my right leg. Damn. My leg felt like a thousand bees had attacked, but I managed to get my hand on the phone by the third ring.

"Hello?" I stammered.

"Joyce? I didn't wake you, did I?" asked Gert.

"Uh. I guess you did," I admitted. "Didn't realize how tired I was. Went to sleep in my chair."

"I'm sorry."

"No, don't be. I need to be up anyway."

"Janet and I decided to go to Ruby Tuesday's for dinner. We wondered if you'd like to come along. Janet has to leave tomorrow morning, and she'd like to spend some time with you too."

"That sounds great. I could use some good company and definitely some good food. When are you going?"

"We thought about five o'clock. Will that work for you?"

I glanced at the clock and saw it was almost four-thirty. "I'll make it work," I said. "I'll be over in a bit."

Oh damn! This was going to be one fast shower, and I'd have to grab something easy to put on. I hobbled to the bathroom. My right leg still felt like it was being attacked with vicious, pointy needles.

At exactly five o'clock, I pressed Gert's doorbell. Janet opened the door and threw her arms around my neck.

"Joyce, I'm so glad to see you," she said, grinning from ear-to-ear. I noticed her hair was a new color.

"Glad to see you too. I love your hair. You look good as a blond."

Janet is nothing like her mother. Gertrude is conservative to the core and wouldn't allow dye near her hair. Janet is unpredictable and more like me than Gert. Maybe that's why she always seems to get her Mom out of the doldrums.

"Thanks. I get bored and have to try something new once in a while. Sometimes it works and sometimes it doesn't," she said, laughing.

She was what we needed: a breath of fresh air. I saw Gert giving me the once-over, but if she disapproved, she didn't say anything. She looked peaceful and unconcerned.

I'd left off the anklets tonight, just in case.

"Well, let's get going." Janet ordered. "I'll drive. You two sit back and relax."

"Sounds like a deal to me," I agreed, as we walked out the door. The rain had stopped, but we had to dodge little puddles on the way to the car.

We had a wonderful time at dinner, with only a short period of sadness when we passed by the notice in the lobby announcing Jake's memorial service on Friday morning. I think we all silently agreed not to let it cast a shadow on our evening.

When we returned, I gave Janet a big hug, and said goodnight to both of them. Janet had to leave for KC early in the morning. I headed for my place with thoughts of a well-needed and restful night of sleep.

At home, I put on my chartreuse PJ's in record time, and slid between the covers. However, as tired as I was, sleep did not answer my call. All I could see in my mind was Jake's memorial notice outlined in gold. My head spun with unanswered questions. There had been no word from Mabel in regard to Bonnie. She'd had time to contact her friend. I wondered what in hell her excuse would be, but I felt certain we were not getting a damn thing from her.

In the morning I'd see if Fannie would give us Bonnie's info. She owed me a favor for helping her brother out of a tight spot, and besides under the circumstances why wouldn't she? She knew Gert and I were Jake's best friends. Pictures of Mabel's gun, Eddie's word to me, the break-ins and a million other things flashed through my head for hours. I awoke at 5:30 feeling like roadkill.

I threw on my robe, staggered to the kitchen, made some coffee, and had just settled in my chair when a knock on the door jolted me back to reality. Recovering enough to shuffle to the peephole, I peeked out and saw Gert in a crisp purple pantsuit. She looked bright and chipper. I almost didn't want to let her in. I knew she was going to ruin my pity party, and I wasn't through wallowing.

"Good morning," I said, pulling open the door. I tried to smile, but it was too much effort. My hair had not yet seen a brush and resembled a red porcupine.

"Looks like someone's a little grumpy this morning," Gert said, as her grin faded a bit.

"Oh, I'm okay. I just had a lousy night." Shape-up, I thought to myself. This is your best friend, the one you need. "Come on in. You want some coffee? I just started mine."

"Sure. I saw Janet off a few minutes ago, so I'm up and out a bit earlier than usual. I could use some more."

I set my cup by my chair and went to the kitchen to get Gert's coffee. In a 'woe-is-me' voice, I said, "I spent almost the entire night thinking about what has gone on the last couple of days. I feel certain Mabel's not going to give us any info about Bonnie. There's something funny about her. I'm not sure what it is, but I'm going to find out if it kills me."

"Oh, Joyce. I think you're overreacting, and for goodness sake, don't use the word 'kill'."

She looked terribly stressed. I felt bad knowing, in only a couple of seconds, I had wiped the smile off my best friend's face.

"You're probably right," I said, forcing myself to look more pleasant, and feeling guilty as hell. "Have you had breakfast yet?"

"No, Janet was going to run through McDonald's, and eat

on her way home."

"Well, finish your coffee while I change into something presentable and we'll go see what they're serving this morning."

At seven fifteen we walked through the sliding doors of the White Dove. We went to the dining room and helped ourselves at the buffet. I saw Nora holding court across the room, thankfully with her back to us. As we sat down, I realized that Nadine, Mabel, and a young man were sitting a short distance away.

"Gert, would you do something for me?"

"I guess it depends on what it is," she said, squinting her eyes at me.

"Nothing dangerous," I said, hoping I was right.

"What is it?"

"Would you ask Mabel to teach you to crochet?"

"Why would I do that?" she asked, giving me a curious look. "I don't want to know how to crochet."

"I know, but please. You don't have to do it more than once. After your lesson is over, just say you don't think it's for you."

She wrinkled her brow, and asked, "What are you getting me into?"

"I just need to know more about Mabel. Does she really do all the handiwork blanketing her house, and why isn't she giving us Bonnie's address?"

"You always make it sound so simple, and it never turns out that way," Gert said, giving her ham a vicious stab. "This better not be one of those times when it goes sour."

Lord I was so thankful she didn't ask, for once, why I didn't do it. I couldn't explain my fear of handwork to anyone. I don't have a clue myself, and it's damned embarrassing for a P.I.

I looked up to see Mabel and her group approaching our table.

"Good morning," said Mabel, with a pleasant smile. "This is Nadine's son, Mark."

Mark was a nice looking young man, dressed in jeans and a t-shirt. I guessed him to be around thirty-five.

We said 'hello', shook hands and all those nice things.

Mabel went on, "I'm sad to say Mark is here to help his mother pack, so she can move in with him and his family."

Mark moved closer and said, "Mom's very upset about Mr. Thompson falling yesterday. Then after I heard about Mr. Robards' murder, I felt I'd rather have her where I can keep an eye on her. Mr. Bennett was nice enough to let her out of her lease." He patted his mother on the back and Nadine placed her hand lovingly on his arm.

"We're sorry to see you go," I said to Nadine. "Especially under the circumstances. This is usually a very quiet and peaceful place. Sorry you had to see it like this."

Nadine gave us a tight smile, but gripped her son's arm a

little tighter and looked anxious to be on her way. Not a very strong woman, I thought to myself. Maybe she had her reasons. Who was I to say?

Mabel stepped a bit closer to me and said, "I'm so sorry. I wasn't able to get an address for Bonnie. My friend must be on the trip to Mexico she's been talking about. I couldn't remember when it was she was going, but it must be now. She's not answering her phone. I wish I could have helped you."

Yeah, the hell you do, I thought, but said, "That's okay. You tried. Maybe there is something else you could do for us though. I was telling Gert about the lovely c-crochet work you have in your place, and she wondered if you might be willing to teach her. She's always wanted to learn," I said. Damn! It was all I could do to mention it. I looked from Gert's pallid face back to Mabel's. I had to give Gert credit. She was doing her best not to give me away.

Mabel's face looked tense. It took her a few seconds to recover, but then she seemed to master a more peaceful look, and said, "Oh, my. I guess I have to confess. I didn't actually do any of the work. It came from my mother-in-law. She gave it all to me when she knew she was dying. My late husband always wanted it on display, so I've just kept it that way."

Did she give you the basket with the gun in it too? I wanted to ask, but managed to keep my big mouth shut.

Mabel looked apologetically at Gert.

"That's okay," said Gert. "I'll find someone else."

Mabel spoke up and said, "Guess we'd better be going."

"Nadine we're sorry to see you leave, but you'll probably feel better with your family. See you later, Mabel."

She waived as they left the room. I felt she would rather run than walk, just in case we thought of anything else to ask her.

When they were out of earshot, I turned to Gert. "Good job, my friend," I said, with a big grin and a pat on her hand. "See, it turned out to be an easy one. You didn't even have to crochet and thanks for keeping up with the right words, so Mabel didn't catch on. I knew she wasn't going to give us the address. There is definitely something weird about that woman. I can understand keeping out a few pieces of your mother-in-law's work, but I'm telling you it's on everything, Gert. And why would she keep the basket and crochet hooks out if she can't use it for anything other than to hide her gun?"

Oh, hell-fire! Damnation! I'd let the cat out of the bag, I thought, and to Gert of all people.

"What? You were setting me up to take lessons from a woman with a gun? Joyce Greenly, how could you do such a thing?" She looked like she wanted to rip my head off. I've never seen her so furious.

"Now, Gertrude, settle down. I'm not sure it was a gun." Can you go to hell for lying to your best friend? But really I can't see any reason Mabel would have shot Gert during a crochet lesson.

"I didn't get a very good look at whatever it was. It may not have been a gun at all." I made a mental note to confess to someone, even though I'm a Baptist.

"But you should have told me," Gert said, giving me the evil eye.

"I know, and I'm sorry. It's just that you get spooked so easily, I didn't want to worry you about something until I was sure what I'd seen."

"Like when you saw my dead body?" she asked, with a growl.

"Oh, Gert, can we just get past this? I promise I will tell you everything from now on, if you just won't freak out on me."

"Okay," she said finally, with furrowed brows and tight lips. "But from now on you tell me the truth. If I can't trust you, I'll be more afraid," she hissed, waving her fork at me.

Guess she had a point there. "You got it. I promise. If I know it, you'll know it." I thought maybe I'd better move on while I was ahead.

"I need to talk to Fannie and see if she can help us. Do you mind if I go on? I'll come by your place later, and let you know if she gives us anything."

"Why are you so hung up on getting her address, other than sending cards or flowers? We'll see her at the service."

"Because I want to see if she can give me more information about Jake. No one seems very clear on who he was, or what he did before he retired. It might help us figure out who his enemies were. We may not have a chance to talk to her in private at the service."

"I definitely want his killer caught, but we're supposed to let the police handle it."

"I'm doing that," I said, not quite truthfully, "but I'd like to make sure they don't miss anything."

"Go ahead. I'll see you later," she said, shaking her head like her friend was a lost cause.

Chapter 9

I asked the young man working at the desk if I could talk to Fannie. She was visible working at her desk behind the glass wall. The clerk rang her extension. She answered and when he relayed my message, she put the phone down and came out to the front desk. I had moved to the end where it would be more private.

"Hi, Joyce. How are you?"

"I'm fine, but I have a favor to ask," I said, lowering my voice.

"What can I do for you?"

"Would you please give me Bonnie, Jake's niece's address, and phone number too, if you have it? Gert and I'd like to send her a card or some flowers."

Dang. I'd have to add this to my confession too, I thought. Being totally truthful doesn't always fit with P.I. work. I'd have to spend next week in church.

"Joyce, we're not supposed to give out other people's information. I don't know," she hesitated. Her blue eyes looked troubled. "Since you were so good to help my brother, I'll do it, but you can't let anyone know. I could lose my job," she said, with a wrinkled brow.

"Fannie, you know Gertrude and I would never do anything to cause you a problem. Besides, since Jake is gone, I can't imagine who would care," I assured her.

"Wait here. I'll be right back," she whispered.

I watched as she went back to her office. She pulled up something on her computer screen and made notes on a pad. A couple of minutes later she was back.

"Here you go," she said, nervously as she handed me a small folded paper.

Louder, so people could hear, I said, "Thanks for the info on the vitamins. I'll give them a try."

"You're welcome. Hope they help," Fannie said, with a look of relief.

I turned to go, and Nora in her bright pink pantsuit and matching heels, was making a beeline toward me. I quickly stuffed Fannie's note into the front pocket of my shoulder bag.

"Joyce, I'm so glad to see you. How are you?"

"I'm fine, but in a big hurry. Can I catch you later?"

"Sure, I guess so," she answered, her eyes asking all kinds of questions: What was I doing that required such speed? What did I know about Jake's murder, and had I heard anything about Eddie?

"See you later," I said, and scooted out the door. Damn it, I don't care if I was rude. Her world revolves around prying every little personal detail from anyone she can get her hands on. To be honest, I was sort of doing the same, but she did it for gossip, and mine was to catch a killer.

I left the building and headed for Gert's. A few minutes

later, we unfolded the note Fannie had given me.

"What the hell?"

"I don't understand," said Gertrude, a look of disbelief on her face. "I thought she lived on Walnut Street."

We stood staring in amazement at the note Fannie had given me. It said: 'Bonnie Edwards, P O Box 928003, Washington, D.C., 20002, Phone: 202-405-5000, ext. 3051.'

"Hell fire! What's the deal? There must be way more to Jake than we were led to believe," I gasped, dropping on the sofa. Gert plopped next to me. I held the paper in front of our faces: as if we stared at it long enough it would say what we had expected and the world would return to normal...it didn't.

"Did he lie to us?" Gert asked, as if the man she'd cared so much for had betrayed her. Her eyes started to glisten.

"Gert, if he did, I'm sure he had a good reason: like trying to stay alive."

"Why did Mabel tell us Bonnie lived on Walnut Street?" Gert asked, looking at me as if I could explain the mess.

"Don't have an answer for that, but I feel for some reason, she didn't want us to talk to Bonnie. Now we need to find out why and how Mabel is involved. Why in hell did it matter to her?"

"I'm glad I didn't have to crochet with that woman." Gert twisted her hands in her lap.

"You realize we have to act normal around her. We can't let her know we suspect her of anything. Is that understood?"

"Yes, yes," Gert replied. "I've been around you long enough, some of your ways are rubbing off on me," she said, as if it was a curse.

I ignored the slight insult and carried on.

"Just because Bonnie lives in Washington DC doesn't mean she has anything to do with the government, but it does make me wonder. There's one way to find out."

Chapter 10

I pulled my phone out, and dialed the number listed on the note.

Two rings later, I heard: "Department of Justice." Hot damn! My fingers were shaking like dry leaves in a hailstorm. It was all I could do to follow the prompts and leave a message for Bonnie Edwards.

I hung up and turned to Gert, "She works at the Department of Justice! Either she's really Jake's niece and it's merely a coincidence, or we are up to our necks in something we weren't prepared for. The Department of Justice manages Witness Protection cases, among other things. We've got to do some digging. If he had connections with the U.S. Marshall's office here, then we can be pretty sure he was in a protection program. Oh, damn-it-to-hell. How are we going to do that?"

"What do you mean 'we,'" Gert yelled. "I've never wanted any part of this. I said, 'Leave it to the police', and I still say that! There is no 'we'."

"Okay, okay. I admit I have kind of dragged you along with me, but I had no idea the government might be involved, and for that matter, we still don't." Gazing at the floor, I said quietly, "I'm sorry, Gert, but if it does turn out to be risky, I'm not sure I can keep you out of it. Everyone knows we're best friends, and you were the one who found Jake. Like it or not you may be stuck with me."

Silence filled the room for several minutes. We sat like mannequins, but our brains were a complete contradiction to our frozen faces. Gert finally spoke up.

"Joyce. I'm sorry. You're a little quick on the trigger, but I know you didn't get us in this mess deliberately. I didn't mean what I said. You know I'll do what I can. I'm just not as fearless as you. Let's hope it's more simple than it appears at this point," she said, putting her hands in a prayerful pose.

"Gertrude, you don't realize how important you are to me. You're my partner and my best friend. I sincerely hope this turns out to be an easy one, but if not, I'll do everything in my power to keep you safe."

"Okay, where do we go from here, boss?" Gert said, with a glint of worry in her eyes.

Before I could answer, we heard the blast of sirens entering the gates of the White Dove again. We rushed to the window. Several people were gathered around Nora's cottage. A few minutes later, a stretcher came rolling down the sidewalk toward her door. Gert and I walked outside to see what had happened. We kept our distance as I've always thought it rude and inconsiderate to jump in the middle of a crowd where you can do nothing except get in the way. There were enough of those out there already.

We heard a loud male voice say, "She said she fell over a flower pot that she put too close to her front door. She thinks her leg might be broken."

I hoped this was an accident and nothing more. Dirt, broken pieces of clay pot, and a tortured geranium had been pushed away from the door.

The paramedics made quick work of loading her onto the gurney.

"Get my shoes," yelled Nora. "And stop wrinkling my clothes," she whimpered. "Oh, it's my own fault," she moaned, as they started to roll away.

She would be fine from the sound of her voice. If she cared more about her clothes and shoes than her injuries, she was probably not near death's door.

I'm sure the paramedics were wondering what in hell kind of retirement center this was, this being their third trip in as many days. Mr. Bennett was trotting just behind the gurney, dutifully carrying Nora's shoes. Was he concerned about how all this carnage might reflect on him, or who knows, maybe he really did care about Nora and her welfare.

Just as we turned to go, I noticed a huge form blending with the small trees behind the fence; it could only be Big Jim. Chills danced up my spine.

The show over, we stepped back into Gertrude's living room. I tried to dismiss the giant image in the leaves.

"Why would she put a flower pot in her doorway?" Gert asked, more to herself than me.

"Just what I was thinking. She said it was her fault, but I

wonder. Nora was in the main building when I left. The pot would have had to been moved after that. Doesn't make sense she would have forgotten it so soon. She said it was her fault, but did she mean moving the pot, or something else?"

"You think someone put it there deliberately?" Gert's eyes were the size of doughnuts.

"Possibly. Someone might have gotten pissed about all her questions and nonstop gossiping. Me for one."

"But you would never hurt her," Gertrude said, in a statement with both a period and a question mark.

"Oh, of course not. You know me better than that. But some people would: especially a killer."

"Mercy," Gert exclaimed, "Do you think that's who did it?"

"I have no way of knowing. She took the blame, but I wonder if she's scared? She has to know, somewhere in her batty brain, that poking her nose in everyone's business might tick some people off. She can't be that clueless."

"I hope she's not hurt too badly," Gert said, as she moved to the sofa and sat down again.

"Can I borrow your phone?"

"What's wrong with yours?" she said, looking at me like maybe I'd finally gone over the edge.

"I want to leave mine open in case Bonnie calls back. We don't want to miss her. You answer if it rings. I want to see how Eddie's doing."

Gert handed over her phone. I Googled Mercy's number

and hit 'call.' The hospital's receptionist answered.

"I'd like to check on Eddie Thompson's condition."

"Let me look him up," she replied, in a kind, sweet voice. Seconds later, she said, "May I ask your name please?"

"Joyce Greenly."

"Ms. Greenly, he is in serious condition, but since you're on the permitted list of visitors, you may see him if you wish. You'll need to bring a picture ID."

"Thank you." I hung up and handed Gert her phone.

Yea! Detective Lancaster actually put me on the list.

"Do you suppose we could be in danger too?" Gert asked softly, as though she wasn't sure she wanted an answer.

"I truly don't know, Gert. We haven't been as obviously nosy as Nora, but we have asked Mabel about Bonnie. We gave a legitimate reason for wanting the information. Guess it boils down to whether or not Mabel is involved, and if she thought we were on to her, or she told someone else."

"Oh," Gert muttered. "I don't like this. What do we do now?"

"I say we lie low for today. If Bonnie calls, maybe that will give us something to go on. If she doesn't, then I guess we'll try and talk to her tomorrow."

"Why don't we put on our jogging clothes, and get away from this miserable situation for a while?" Gert piped up. "How about the Nature Center? We could use the exercise, and we might see some interesting birds or animals. It would have to be better than this."

"You're so right, Gert. Let's get out of here."

We changed and headed to the car, hoping the gentle breeze would help turn our thoughts from murder to nature.

The Ozarks hills are one of the best places in the world to calm and sooth frazzled nerves. We arrived at the nature center, and decided to forgo the small information center and museum. The wooded trail that wound down the hill was our target. In minutes we were enveloped in nature at its finest. Several small creatures peeked from behind rocks and trees along the way.

Our walk was very enjoyable and I did feel more relaxed and at peace. However, the giant form looming in the leaves was still haunting me.

We left, and headed home. I hesitated to bring it up, and diminish Gert's refreshed spirit, but, damn, I just don't have an 'off' button.

"Gertrude, it's clear you don't seem as concerned about Jim Landis as I do, but would you mind if I borrow your car? Mine is so conspicuous. I want to follow him home, and see where he lives. I need to know more about him. Maybe some of his neighbors will be in their yards, or walking. If I can strike up a conversation, and work in some questions just right, maybe they won't think anything of it. If I don't get it right, someone might tell him I was snooping; don't want that. Cross your fingers it works as planned."

"Joyce, you know you're welcome to use my car, but be cautious. All sorts of things could go wrong with your plan. If he is evil, you could be putting yourself in great danger. Be extra careful, for goodness sake."

"You know I will, Gertrude."

At four-thirty, I stopped in the snack room, and got a ham sandwich and a bottle of water. I headed to Gert's car, and waited for Big Jim to get in his pickup. I was pretty sure he got off at 5:00, but knew it could vary. I was debating on whether to take a bite of the sandwich, when his huge frame came ducking out the employee entrance. I dropped my food on the seat, and started Gert's car.

Jim climbed in his pickup, started the engine, and rolled toward the street. I let him get to the corner before I pulled out. There was a four-way stop there. I hoped he would turn and not continue straight ahead, so he wouldn't see me come out of the lot in his rearview mirror. He turned left. Super. I followed as far behind as possible. I didn't want to lose him at a light. If he was going to Lowes or a grocery store, this could be a tedious tail job. "Please go home," I whispered.

His next turn was into a neighborhood. "Hot Damn. Maybe he heard me!" I now stayed back a little further, as I was more noticeable on a side street with fewer cars. Luckily, he went only a couple of blocks before he turned into the driveway of a cozy little house.

I quickly pulled over, parked, and tied a flowered headscarf over my bright red hair. Big Jim went into the house, without so much as a glance in my direction. I was both surprised and concerned that he lived less than a mile from the White Dove…that would make sneaking around a hell of a lot easier. He could walk if necessary.

Dressed in a gray knit shirt, and pants, I left the car, and walked down the sidewalk, as if I was out for an afternoon walk. A man was pulling weeds from his flowerbed, across the street and one house down from Big Jim's. He was exactly what I needed. Now if I could strike up a conversation, without it looking contrived.

That was not a problem. Just as I was about to say, 'Hello', the man accidentally flipped a small rock on to the sidewalk, just as my foot reached for the same space. The rock must have been clinging to roots of the weed he'd pulled.

I was so engrossed in how to start a conversation with this strange man, I didn't see, nor would I have had time to react to the obstacle. My foot landed on it, and somewhat like a cow on ice, I landed smack in the middle of the man's columbines. They didn't survive my assault. My left knee hit the edge of the sidewalk, so now both my knees were in need of repair.

A strong hand grabbed my arm, and helped pull me out of the dirt.

"Are you okay, Lady?"

"Oh, yes. I'm so sorry I've crushed your flowers." My knee hurt like hell, but I couldn't mention that after what I'd just done to his plants.

"Do you need to sit down? I'll get a chair off the porch. That was my fault. I threw that rock right in front of you."

I grabbed his shirt as he turned to go. "No, no. I'm fine. I should have been watching where I was going. It's just that I was looking at a huge guy across the street. He was so tall! Do you know him?"

"Not real well. Think his name is Jim, or something. He doesn't mix with the neighbors much. Kind of odd, or maybe he just isn't a people person. You're right he is really big: almost giant like. His mother, Anne is very nice, and she's only about five foot four. He must have gotten his height from his dad: never seen him."

"So, he lives with his mother?"

"Yep. Are you sure you're okay?"

"Oh, yes. I'm fine. I'm so sorry about your flowers."

"It was my fault as much as yours. You certainly didn't do it on purpose. I have some just like them at the side of the house. I'll just move them around here so people can see them better. Don't worry about it."

"Well, good. I'm glad you have more. I was going for a longer walk, but think I'll call it quits, and head back home while I'm still upright," I said, with a grin,

"It was nice meeting you…"

"Grace," I lied, just in case someone from the house across the street asked.

"George," he said.

We shook hands, and I walked back toward the car, trying not to limp.

Well, hell! That didn't go as planned, but at least I know where he lives, and he lives with his mother. 'Odd', George had said. What exactly did that mean? I pondered on that all the way home: that and what my knee looked like under my ripped pants.

Chapter 11

Friday morning arrived with a cloudless sky. A humming bird flitted from bloom to bloom in my petunia pot. I sipped my coffee and thought how Jake would have enjoyed this peek at nature.

Minutes later, I saw Gertrude heading toward my door. I set my cup on the counter and went to open the door.

"Good morning," I greeted her, opening it before her finger pushed the bell.

"Oh, goodness. You startled me. Are you ready for breakfast?"

"I am. I've been sipping coffee and admiring the beautiful day.

I hate this is the day we have to say goodbye to Jake, but on the other hand, it's a day he would have loved. Maybe it's fitting that the sun is shining and the birds are singing."

"It is sad," Gert replied. "But you're right. He would have enjoyed this."

As we headed to the dining room, we saw one of the staff going into Nora's cottage with a food tray.

"She must be home. That's good," Gert remarked.

"Yes, it is, but something must be wrong if she's not going to the dining room.

We walked through the sliding doors. Wonderful smells of

bacon, sweet rolls and coffee kissed our noses. My stomach growled embarrassingly loud. We entered the dining room and headed for the buffet. Part of the room had been closed off with folding walls.

I'm sure Gert noticed too, but we both tried to ignore it, and what we knew was almost certainly behind the gray structure. I had filled her in on Big Jim last night when I returned her keys. We discussed that a bit. The food was good: but it was hard to appreciate it, this morning. The atmosphere inside was drastically different than outside: no birds chirping, no bees, or fragrant flowers.

Mabel was eating with a lady whose name I think is Evelyn. She lives near Mabel, so it seemed reasonable. I guess. Who the hell knows?

Just then, Mr. Bennett squeezed his way through a small opening between the wall and the partition we were all trying not to see. He glanced around the room a minute or two. His eyes seemed to focus on Mabel for a few seconds. Did that mean anything? I think several people saw him before he ducked back inside. I needed to be careful and not start connecting people with every fly that buzzed through. Besides, Bennett had been nothing but kind to us.

"Do you want to walk for a bit?" I asked Gert, as we pushed away from the table.

"That sounds nice. A little fresh air would be great."

I glanced at my watch and said, "It's only 8:30. We have

plenty of time before we need to change clothes."

We walked slowly; my knees were fussing. Both of us tried to relax as much as possible, but the service was looming in our heads. We admired flowers, squirrels, bees and chipmunks. The grounds were a picture-perfect view of nature this morning. We were jolted out of our pleasant walk when we realized we had meandered our way to within six feet of the walk that led to the gazebo. The hateful crime tape was still up. When would they take that odious stuff down?

We stood frozen like statues on the edge of a cliff.

"Damn, I didn't realize we'd come this far."

"Me either," said Gert, looking as if she wanted to run.

"Wait," I said. "We'll have to get used to this. If we want to help find Jake's killer, we may have to face worse things. While we're here, let's take another look at the lake. Do you think anyone could have come in this way?" I asked.

"I don't see how it would be possible," she replied, shaking her head.

"Me either. I think it was just a stupid 'red herring', an attempt to make it look like someone did…stupid being the operative word. It's just not possible."

"Do you suppose the police think it could have happened that way?" Gert asked.

"You know what I think? I think they just gave us that impression to get us off the trail."

Chapter 12

A glance at my phone showed it was time to get ready for Jake's service.

We parted to change for the funeral. At nine thirty, we entered the memorial service thirty minutes early. We were hoping to meet Jake's niece. There were a few people seated already. Funny how the older we get, the earlier we seem to show-up.

A spray of beautiful white roses lay across the dark gray casket. They were the only flowers in the room, except for a large plastic plant that was probably provided by the funeral home. A note had been posted at the bottom of the memorial announcement asking for donations to a children's home in New Jersey rather than flowers. Gert and I had already sent our checks, since we had seen the request on the funeral notice posted in the lobby.

I noted the usual ribbon saying "UNCLE" was missing. Why? There were no unfamiliar women in the gathering crowd. Where was Bonnie?

Seconds before the service began, Detective Lancaster and two men I hadn't seen before seated themselves near the back. Who the hell are those two? I wondered, not mentioning them to Gertrude. She looked more stressed with each passing minute.

A recorded hymn started. The service had begun. Gert gripped my hand. It was a nice funeral conducted by a minister from a nondenominational church. I was pretty sure Jake had not had any affiliation with it, but the preacher did a good job even if he didn't know the deceased. As the memorial ended, we both wiped tears from our cheeks. It was so final now. We would never see our friend again. The casket was closed, and I was glad of that.

It was announced that Jake would be flown to a cemetery in New Jersey where several of his family members were buried.

We stood and filed toward the door as "Amazing Grace" drifted through the air. We were just passing Detective Lancaster, when he leaned in and whispered in my ear.

"Would you two ladies please meet us at police headquarters in thirty minutes? We need to talk to you." He smiled and fell in behind us.

"Holy hell!" I said to Gert, as we got far enough outside so no one could hear.

"Joyce, what a thing to say when just leaving Jake's service!"

"It doesn't have anything to do with that," I answered. "Detective Lancaster just asked us to meet him, and whoever the other two men are, at police headquarters."

"Whatever for?" Gert asked, looking shocked. "They don't think we had anything to do with Jake's murder, do they?"

Twenty-eight minutes later we turned into the parking lot on Chestnut Expressway. Several black and whites were mixed with a few black, unmarked SUVs. Our hearts were beating a little faster than usual as we parked and headed toward the door.

Detective Lancaster met us just inside, and escorted us to a small room. The other two gentlemen got to their feet as we entered.

"Can we offer you some coffee or water to drink? Don't believe what you see on TV. Our coffee's not as bad as they make it out to be," the detective said, with a smile.

We both declined. I always have to pee at least five times for each cup of coffee, and this didn't feel as if it was the sort of meeting where one could ask to be excused a number of times.

"Ladies, this is Agent Jack Niger, with the FBI, and Deputy Sam Brighton from the US Marshal Service."

We shook hands. They seemed to already know who we were as our names were not mentioned.

"Ladies, I feel I may owe you an apology for keeping you in the dark, but it was my attempt to protect you. Mrs. Greenly, knowing you, you may already be aware of some of what's going on," the detective stated, looking at me sternly.

"You mean like, Jake didn't have a niece named Bonnie, and he was in the Witness Protection Program?"

"Maybe we need to hire her," exclaimed Deputy Brighton,

with a grin.

"We also know the killer didn't come through the damn lake, and I suspect you didn't think so either…Sir." Oops! I was getting a little too mouthy for my own good. I needed to show a little respect. Couldn't risk losing my visiting privileges with Eddie.

"Anything else you want to tell us?" asked Agent Niger.

"Nope. Guess it's your turn," I replied, more subdued than usual.

"Mrs. Bush?"

"No, no," answered Gert, shaking her head and looking at the floor.

"Obviously, our attempt to protect and shelter you has been totally ineffective," commented Detective Lancaster. "How about we work together on a limited basis? As long as you follow the rules," he added.

I nodded my head. Gertrude's nod was barely visible.

"He was under my watch," said Deputy Brighton. "I feel responsible, and you can bet I won't rest until I find the low-life who did this. Jake was a good man," he finished in a quiet, subdued voice. He turned and stared out the window: his back to the room.

The man obviously meant what he said. I knew how he felt. Only my language might have been a little stronger.

"Have you talked to Eddie yet?" I asked Detective Lancaster.

"We tried today, but he still seemed out of it, and even a bit scared of us. If someone did push him he probably doesn't know who to trust. We were wondering, Mrs. Greenly if you would see if he will talk to you? But, only if you agree to our terms," he added. "You have to tell us exactly what he says."

"I have to interject here," growled Agent Niger, "This deal doesn't have my blessing. This is a job for trained law enforcement. Not two elderly ladies."

What a jerk! It was all I could do not to punch his smug face with my senior fist.

"Mrs. Greenly does have P.I. experience, Jack. We're not going to ask them to do anything dangerous; just some light surveillance, and keeping a lookout. Things we can't do in that setting without being noticed. Extra eyes are always appreciated."

Agent Niger looked disgusted. He threw both hands in the air and said, "It's on you. I want it on record that I'm playing no part in this idiotic plan."

"Understood," said Detective Lancaster.

"Fine by me," added Deputy Brighton.

I could have sworn there was the faintest look of satisfaction on the deputy's face as he turned to look at Agent Niger. Had they had differences before?

"You two are making a big mistake expecting aging women to do our job," Agent Niger said, with a sneer. "I want no part of this." He grabbed a fat folder and left the room.

Aging! He had said that like we were two steps from the grave. Gert and I looked at each other like we'd just been slapped. Gert's face actually turned pink, and I could see she was furious. I was seething.

"I'm sorry," Detective Lancaster said. "I'm not sure Agent Niger understands how capable you are. I don't want you or any other citizen getting hurt, but talking to Eddie and keeping your eyes open will be a big help to us. Under different circumstances, I probably wouldn't ask you to help. But, I know you are going to do it anyway, and I can't do much about that. Just promise you will not take any chances or do anything foolish on your own. Keep in touch and let me know if you see or hear anything that might help. Do you have time to see Eddie on your way home?"

"Sure," I answered. "We were planning to do that anyway."

"Here are my cards," said Deputy Brighton, handing one to each of us. "Call me anytime you can't get the detective, have questions, or need help."

"Thanks, we'll do that," I said, with a smile. He seemed like a stand-up guy.

"We'll report later on what happens with the visit to Eddie," I said, as we headed to the door.

Chapter 13

We walked stiffly and silently across the parking lot to my car and opened the doors in unison.

Gert's fanny had hardly touched the seat when she said, "Joyce you tell me what to do and we'll make that damn Agent Niger look like a fool!" she exclaimed, quickly followed by, "I'm sorry for the language, but how dare he insinuate we are two old bags of useless trash. We'll show him," she said, folding her arms across her chest.

Hearing "damn" come out of Gert's mouth was so shocking; it took me a second to reboot. In all the years we'd known each other this was a first. She had to be steaming.

"Bless you, Gert. I agree. He's a pompous ass, and I swear if it's within our power, we are going to make him eat those words. Let's go see if Eddie can tell us anything."

We drove across town to Mercy's huge parking lot. I purposely passed up empty spaces to park near the back. I was in an "I'll prove I'm not an 'old fart' mode." Gert must have felt the same. She said nothing about our long hike to the front door.

"I'll have a latte in the coffee shop while you talk to Eddie. Take your time. I've got my word search book in my purse," said Gert.

"Thanks. Wish me luck," I said, with a pat on her shoulder.

I crossed the lobby to the front desk and asked for Eddie's room number. I had to show my ID as the lady said his visitors were restricted, which, of course, I already knew. Eddie was on the fifth floor.

When the elevator door opened, I saw a police officer outside a room at the far end of the hall. Must be the place. After trudging what seemed half a mile, I saw the number '545' by the door next to the officer: Eddie's room.

"Can I help you?" the officer said, when he realized I had stopped beside him.

"Yes, my name is Joyce Greenly. I'm here to see Eddie."

I had to show my ID again, but soon stood by Eddie's bed. He was a pitiful sight. Bruises had now formed. They showed where each part of his body had bounced brutally off walls and steps. His face was swollen and misshapen, eyes closed in irregular shapes. It was hard to say if he was awake or asleep. Most of his head, arms, and one leg were wrapped in plaster and bandages. Oh, hell! This was going to be hard.

I was pretty sure he was asleep, and couldn't bring myself to bother such a pathetic soul. I started to back away, when he raised one of the only fingers not tied down and seemed to be trying to motion me to come closer. I moved closer and bent toward his face, not sure he could really see who I was. Did he think I was a nurse?

"J-Jce," he whispered through cracked lips.

"Yes, Eddie it's Joyce. I came by to see if I can help you," I whispered, not really wanting the officer to hear in case he had any "Niger" connections. "Can you talk?" I asked the eye that seemed to be looking at me.

"Bit," he said in a barely audible, shaky voice.

"Do you know who pushed you?"

"B,brotr."

"Are you saying "brother"? I asked.

"Es."

"Eddie, I'm sorry. Can you tell me whose brother?"

"B-b."

It was plain to see the effort of those few words had taken their toll. The eye that had been looking at me was now dim and unfocused.

"Eddie?"

He didn't answer. The machines flashing and making dips above his head indicated he was still alive, but it was clear he had used all the energy he had to offer for now. I placed my hand softly on his chest and whispered, "I'll be back later, goodbye for now."

"That didn't take long. Was he asleep?" Gertrude asked, as I entered the coffee shop, and approached her table.

I noticed she was wearing her hearing aids: maybe getting ready for battle. Good girl.

"Let me get a coffee, and I'll tell you about it."

Cup in one hand, I pulled out a chair with the other and sat down. I told Gert what had happened; which didn't take long since I didn't get much, and didn't have an idea in hell what Eddie was trying to tell me.

"Brother and B-b?" Gert said, staring at me with a look as blank as the space in my head. Do you suppose he was trying to say brother again or a name?"

"Couldn't tell."

"Does that mean anything to you?" she asked.

"Not a damn thing. I'm not even sure he knew what he was saying, but he did know who I was, so I think he was trying to tell me something. I thought he didn't have any family. Guess we need to start by finding out if he has a brother.

"Well if he does have a brother, why would he want to kill him? That doesn't make sense."

"You're right, Gert. We have to start there though. It's all we have. I'll have to report to Det. Lancaster. He can probably find out about Eddie's family." I pulled out my phone to call, but hospitals are notorious for bad cell service. I had no bars at all. "Guess I'll have to wait until we get to the car."

I finished my coffee and we headed out. What had seemed like a show of power and defiance earlier, we very soon realized, had not been a good idea. We were both wearing heels since we had come straight from Jake's funeral. Normally we wear tennis shoes or something flat, at least. It was bad enough for Gert, but I had walked through the hospital, down the long hall to Eddie's room and back down the same hall. My feet were killing me, and my knees throbbed. Gertrude was definitely not walking as briskly as she had on the way in.

By the time we made it to the car, we had slowed to more of a shuffle than what could be called a legitimate walk. We opened the doors and plopped into the seats in silence. If we mentioned our throbbing feet it would be acknowledging a weakness, and we had none.

I got out my cell, which now had three and a half bars instead of the barely visible dot in the hospital. A few minutes later Det. Lancaster said he would check on Eddie's siblings. I was anxious to hear what he would come up with. Even one sibling would be another thread to pull. There were just too many questions to be answered, too many strings to unravel.

We were too tired to speak on our way home. Friends don't have to keep a conversation going non-stop. My head, however, was twirling with a myriad of thoughts. Mine, at the moment, were of a magnificent bucket filled with Epsom salts and warm water. My feet were pleading for the soothing comfort it would provide. I suspect Gertrude had similar thoughts. Of course, for both of us, the thoughts of Jake's murder came before our aching feet.

The two of us used every thread of bravery we processed to walk slowly through the lobby of the White Dove and sign in. We tried not to limp on our way to the automatic doors and toward our cabins. I wondered if we actually pulled off the charade. Probably not.

Chapter 14

Outside, with no one in sight, all bets were off. It took us about two seconds to remove the offending leather destroying our swollen feet.

"I'm going to go rest a bit," said Gert, sounding exhausted.

"Same here," I answered. She took the left fork in the sidewalk and I took the right. It was great to walk barefoot, but I'm sure we still looked like two old dogs returning from a romp in a thorn field.

I was limping by Nora's cabin, second down the path, when I heard a small pebble bounce across her porch. Startled, I looked at her front door and was surprised to see her peeking through a slight opening at the front door. She was holding her finger in front of her lips in a gesture clearly saying to be quiet. As our eyes met, she pointed to a flowerpot sitting just off the edge of her porch. I took a closer look at the pot. It contained a small marigold plant, and in the soil at the edge of the container, laid a folded piece of green paper. My eyes went back to her, and she was nodding her head as if the note was for me. Casually reaching down to touch the flower as if admiring it, I palmed the piece of paper. A quick glance at her door told me that was what she wanted. It was now closed.

"What the hell?" The urge to read the note was almost unbearable. But with all the 'cloak and dagger' on Nora's part, it was probably not a good idea. Anything that kept Nora from talking must be significant.

I was one cabin from mine when it happened. SQUISH! I knew instantly what it was. Goose poop, damn it to hell. It's bad enough to step in it with your shoes on, but with pantyhose ... Yuck, Hell, Damn! Usually I keep an eye out for it, but the note tucked between my fingers had erased my good sense. I limped the rest of the way with my left foot and right heel. The thought of feeling that nasty goop go any further between my toes was more than I could bear. It brought memories of doing the same sort of dance through my grandmother's chicken yard when I was a child. Most people who've grown up around chickens are familiar with this insult, but how much more could my feet take today? This was just wrong.

Inside, doing my "poop" hobble to the bathroom, I put on some rubber gloves, pulled off the pantyhose, and quickly deposited then in the trash. Washing them would not remove the hateful memory and contamination. With a paper towel, soap and hot water, I carefully cleaned between my toes. Have I mentioned how I hate geese, chickens, and pigeons? The list goes on. If they leave anything I can step in, they're on it.

Soon I sat in my favorite chair with my feet in an old dishpan filled with Epsom salts and warm water. I was practically purring, when I noticed the green note on the table next to me. Damn! It should have been the first thing I looked at when I came through the door. I'd let goose poop run me off the rails.

I snatched up the paper and unfolded it.

"Meet me at Leong's tonight at 7:00. We can't go together. I will be in disguise. Please come alone, and don't tell anyone."

What the hell? This sounded like Sherlock Holmes and Dr. Watson. I knew she hadn't been as chatty since she broke her leg, but she must really be on to something, scared, or both. Damn! Maybe we should all be careful. The way she was acting, she must think her place is bugged. Shit! Maybe mine is too. Maybe Gert's as well. What the devil is going on? I was scaring myself, but also feeling mad as hell. STOP IT, Joyce. Just the same, it wouldn't hurt to see if Detective Lancaster could have someone check our places out.

Nora said to come alone and not tell anyone. I wasn't used to keeping things from Gert, especially after today when she had pretty much jumped on the bandwagon.

A few seconds later the phone rang, and my problem was solved.

"Joyce", Gert said, "Do you mind if we don't meet for dinner tonight? I'm worn to a frazzle. Think I'll make myself a sandwich and go to bed early."

"That's fine," I answered, quite relieved. "I totally understand. "We've had a long day."

"I knew you'd probably be tired too. See you for breakfast

in the morning."

    "Get some rest. See you tomorrow."

Chapter 15

I was so relieved. I don't think I could have lied to Gert, even if it meant violating Nora's orders. I looked at the clock, and decided I could soak another fifteen minutes.

The thought of going to Leong's was exciting to me, even if my feet and knees were protesting. Leong's has been Springfield's claim to fame in the culinary world for many years. The story, as I recall, was that a doctor had liked Mr. Leong's cooking so well, he paid him to come to America and cook for him. His most famous dish was Cashew Chicken, a divine combination of fried, small chunks of chicken, oyster sauce, cashews and a sprinkle of chopped green onion. I'm not sure just how he came to have his own restaurant, but he did, and it was packed for years. Most came for the cashew chicken. Many people have tried to duplicate it, but none have been able to capture the essence of his creation.

Mr. Leong is elderly, but still helping out. His son has taken over for the most part, using his dad's recipes. It's as good as ever.

Stop drooling, Joyce, and get back to reality. Since Nora is coming in disguise, should I do the same? Surely she would have said so, if that were needed. I decided not to do it anyway. Why did she feel she needed to hide herself?

I dried my feet with some paper towels, which I stuffed in

the trash, poured the water down the toilet and flushed. Disgusting! A good hot shower should take care of any lingering poop molecules.

An hour and a half later, I was sitting in a tall booth at Leong's, facing the door. If Nora was in disguise, how was she going to hide her broken leg, and the knee walker she had been using? I watched the door for what seemed an eternity, but was actually twenty minutes. The waitress had brought me some water and asked three times if I was ready to order. Telling her I was waiting on someone, only kept a smile on her face through the second request.

To my surprise, Mabel came through the front door just as the girl was leaving my table. Yikes! Quickly lowering my head I pretended to search for something in my purse on the seat beside me. Would she recognize my back, and was it a problem if she did? Fortunately, a large potted plant partially hid me from view as she walked to the back counter of the restaurant. As I peeked through the leaves, she was casually gazing around as if she had nothing on her mind. A few minutes later, after speaking to a waitress, she paid and carried what appeared to be a food order toward the front door. Why didn't she use the drive-through? I stuck my head in the plant again, as she glanced around the room on her way out. Damn, that was close. At least I don't think she saw me. Since Nora gave no clues as to why she was coming in disguise it was impossible to know if Mabel seeing me would have been okay, or a disaster.

Ten minutes later, I was about to give up and place a to-go order, when a lady I'd never seen before, walked up.

"Are you Joyce Greenly?" she asked.

"Yes."

"Nora is waiting for you in the car. We will order some food for you when you get there."

"And exactly who are you," I asked, wondering what in the hell was going on.

"I'm, Christy Long, her attorney. I'm acting as an Uber driver tonight, so we don't attract attention. Sorry we're late," she whispered. "Here is a note from, Nora."

She handed me a small piece of green paper, identical to the one from the flowerpot.

"Joyce, I can't come in. Christy, will explain."

"Let me leave, and then you follow in a minute or two. Look for a green Toyota Camry with an Uber sign. We're on the east side of the lot," Nora's attorney said. She left quickly, and I followed two minutes later.

I left a generous tip for the poor girl who had tried to help me for the past forty minutes.

This was just plain weird. I had not seen this coming. I found the car, and the Uber driver, attorney, got out and opened the back door for me, as if I were a customer.

"Joyce, I'm so sorry we couldn't get you sooner," said Nora. She was adorned with a blond wig, and enough make-up to pass for a hooker. "There was no way to hide my broken leg, so we had to do it this way. I didn't want anyone to recognize me through the car window, so I left with a large scarf draped over my head, pulled it off in the car, and will get rid of the make-up and wig before I go back home."

Not bad for a nosy, stuck-up gossip, I thought, and then quickly chastised myself. She was scared, and probably for good reason the way things had been going.

"What would you like to eat?" Nora asked.

"Cashew Chicken," I answered, wondering why anyone would order anything else, but she and her attorney did. There's no accounting for taste.

Her attorney called and placed the order, and Nora apologized for us having to eat in the car.

"I had thought maybe Christy could bring me in using the wheelchair, as we did when we left the White Dove. But then when we saw Mabel driving through the parking lot, I didn't want to take any chances. I don't know whom I can trust. Oh, Joyce. I'm petrified! Someone is trying to hurt me, and I don't know why. I didn't leave that pot in front of my door. Someone else did. I only said I did, hoping to make them think I was getting the idea that I should stop asking questions about Jake. At least, I guess that's what it's about. I can't think of anything else I've done. I'm almost sure my cottage is bugged, and when I come home, things have been moved. Probably just to let me know they've been there, and can come and go when they please."

"I was pretty sure you didn't leave that plant where you would trip over it."

Christy started the car and headed toward the drive-thru.

"Do you have any friends or family you could stay with for a while?" I asked.

"Not really," she answered, sadly. "I'm pretty much the last of my family. I didn't have any children. I have a niece, but she isn't the type that you can call up and invite yourself over for a week or two."

"I would have her stay at my house, said Christy, but my sister's at mine. She just got a divorce, and has two small children who would drive Jesus nuts."

"You know mine and Gert's places were broken into also?" I asked

Nora nodded she did. "Have things been moved, like mine?"

"I don't think so. Haven't noticed anything. Maybe they, he, or she knows Detective Lancaster is talking to us, and they're being a bit more cautious. One minute I think it has to be someone at the White Dove and the next I feel that's not possible. Most of us have been there for at least a year or two, and several are not in shape to do anything like what's been happening."

"I want Nora to talk to the police, but she won't, said Christy, pulling up to the drive through window.

Nora and I sat quietly as Christy retrieved our order and put it in the seat next to her.

"We need to find somewhere to eat besides this lot. Any ideas," she asked.

"How about one of the hospital parking lots," I suggested. "I see people doing that often. Probably have friends or family who have been there awhile, and need a break from cafeteria food and the depressing atmosphere."

"That will work," she replied, as she handed our drinks back to us, then pulled away from the window.

We were soon parked in a space not far from where Gert and I had been earlier in the day. Christy, after a bit of shuffling, passed the proper food to each of us.

Nora's hands were shaking like a scared rabbit. She unwrapped her plastic utensils, but sat with them in her hands making no attempt to open her food container.

Feeling a little guilty, I dug into mine like a starving wolf. Oh, Lord, it was so good. After a few bites and watching Nora trembling and still not eating, I felt compelled to do what I should have done already…ask some questions, do my job: not one I'd asked for, but one that seemed to be stuck to me like flypaper.

"Nora, do you have any idea why you would be someone's target? What did you do before the flower pot incident?" I could see her face in the glow of one of the security lights. Her eyes were those of a bunny caught in a trap.

"I'm not sure," she said, in a soft whisper. "I know I talk a lot more than I should, and ask too many questions, but if I did anything that would upset someone, I have no idea what it could have been," she answered, rubbing the corner of her still unopened food container. "I don't know if you can help me or not, but you're the only one I trust. Do you think you can?" she asked, with a tremble in her lips.

"You know I will do what I can, but since I have no idea at this point what or who we're involved with, I can't make any promises. Who did you talk to the morning before the flower pot incident?"

"I had breakfast with Lucy. Mabel stopped by our table for a bit, and George Johnson was there."

"Did you ask any questions about Jake or Eddie?"

"I'm sure I probably did. That's all everyone was talking about."

"Nora, was there anything specific or new in the conversation, or did you ask any of them any sort of prying questions?"

"Lord, I'm not sure. I remember some talk about Jake's niece, and of course, Eddie, but that's about all."

"Did anyone act agitated or nervous about a particular subject?"

"I don't know," Nora said, with a sniffle in her voice. "I know people think I'm nosy, and stuck-up," she choked out with a full-blown sob. "Probably a lot of people don't like me, but I don't mean to come across as being better than others," she blubbered. "No one understands how I grew up. We were practically homeless, hand-me down clothes, and very little to eat. I was lucky enough to marry a well to do, hard-working man. He turned my life around. But I'm sure I still come across totally different than I mean to. I just want to make friends, but realize now I've done just the opposite. PLEASE don't tell anyone," she sobbed. "I'm so ashamed."

Well, I felt like the heap of goose poop I'd stepped in earlier, thinking back about all the ugly things I'd said about her. Damn it to hell!

Christy and I both chimed in that her secret was safe with us.

"I'm so sorry, Nora. But being poor is nothing to be ashamed of. It's the way you treat other people that's important, and I apologize for being one of the jerks who was irritated and probably unkind. I didn't realize who you were under that smoke-screen."

"I also have to admit, Nora, that I thought you were a little stuck-up," Christy said. "I'm so sorry."

"No, neither of you are at fault," Nora whispered. "I'm the guilty one. I tried to act like I was better than everyone else. I knew what I was doing, and realized I didn't have any real friends because of my behavior, but my pride kept me from doing anything different. I've thought of little else in the past two days. I'm so ashamed."

"How about we start fresh. Don't worry about the past and we'll all start over. However, until we find out what is going on, it would probably be better if we act as usual. You should keep a low profile, and I will avoid you. If you need me, put a note in the pot and I'll watch for it."

"I can do that," answered Nora. "I'll probably have to leave any notes after dark. Do you have any idea at all who could be at the bottom of this?"

"I wish I did. Has Eddie ever mentioned to you if he had any family?"

"It seems like he may have mentioned a brother, but I don't have a clue where he lives, or where Eddie's from for that matter. He was never very friendly to me."

My heart skipped a beat at the word "brother."

"No one seems to know much about him or Jake," I told her. "What info I get seems to contradict itself."

"Nora, I have to tell you, I know you want me to keep this all hush, hush, but you have to let me include Gertrude. She's helping me investigate, and her word is gold. If I ask her not to tell something, you couldn't get it out of her with a 30-30. Are you good with that?"

"I sort of thought it would go that way. I know you're very close. I'm not thrilled for anyone else to know my story, but if you say that's the way it has to be, then I guess it's okay."

"Thanks, Nora. I appreciate you understanding. She and I work differently, but we make a good team. Now, when did you first feel something was wrong?"

"Really, not until the flower pot incident. For some reason I felt a little tense and nervous the evening before, but I told myself it was because of Jake and Eddie. Maybe it was. This has been a h-horrible week," she stammered, as she stuffed her food and utensils back in the Leong's bag.

"That it has been. You said things had been moved in your cottage. What kind of things?"

"Random things: salt and peppershakers in the bedroom, a pillow in the bathtub, bra in the kitchen sink. Things that don't make sense at all. Things just to scare the hell out of me, and let me know I'm not safe. I'm not positive my place is bugged, but obviously someone has had the opportunity to do so. I'm sorry for dragging you into this, Joyce, but I didn't know who else to turn to, and since you have private eye experience, I felt you were my best bet. And, as I said before, I feel you can be trusted," she said in a soft, fading whisper. I'm afraid to report it to the police. It might make it worse, and they wouldn't be there to protect me."

I had kept taking small bites as we talked. Now finished, I put my trash in a larger bag. "Nora, I'll do everything I can to help. I'll spread the word that you aren't feeling well, and won't be out and about for a few days. Hopefully, that will get them to back off."

"In case your place is bugged, Gert and I will stop by your place on our way to breakfast tomorrow. We'll ask how you are feeling, etc. Just tell us you aren't feeling great, and think you will rest for a few days. If someone is listening, or watching, it will back up my story, and shouldn't cause problems for any of us. Okay?"

"Okay. Oh, thank you so much, Joyce. You don't know how alone I've felt."

"Don't thank me yet, Nora, but you do have a friend, and I will do what I can. You'd better eat that food when you get home," I said, smiling at her. It felt as if I was actually seeing her for the first time.

Christy dropped me off at my car, which I had parked across the street in a strip mall. It's hard to hide my sleek, red ride, but I'll never give it up. I drove to the White Dove and parked across the street where I could see Nora, now minus the wig and make-up work her way out of the fake Uber. With Christy's help, she got on her knee walker and entered the building. Christy carried Nora's take-out bag and I assume, helped her to her door. It wasn't a stretch of imagination to believe an Uber driver would go out of their way to help, since they are private cars.

I thought it might be best, if Nora was right, and someone was watching, that I should wait a bit before returning home. My feet had swollen again after sitting so long, but there was no way I was taking off even one shoe. I swear I could still feel that crap.

Chapter 16

This would be a good time to fill in Detective Lancaster. It was past business hours, if detectives have those. I dialed his number.

"Detective Lancaster," came his familiar voice.

"This is Joyce Greenly. I have some new information."

After a brief conversation, he advised me that tomorrow they would send a woman, disguised as a nurse. She was an expert in finding listening devices. Would I please let Nora know to expect her so they could carry on a normal conversation as the agent was checking? I agreed and hung up.

I made a quick trip to Walmart. Parked as close to the door as possible, and bought myself the softest pair of flip-flops they had, a note pad and a package of green binder clips. In the car, I wrote a message, and explained the situation to Nora. On the way to my cabin, I dropped it in her flowerpot, and continued on in my new cushiony shoes.

Gert was at my door early the next morning: all bright and cheerful. I'm sure she expected us to head to the dining room for breakfast, but I motioned her to come in and have a seat.

"What's wrong?" she asked, looking concerned.

"I need to fill you in on what happen last night."

With Gert up to date, we headed to the dining room, with a quick stop at Nora's. We went through the arranged brief conversation at her door.

"Thanks for checking on me," Nora said, but I haven't been feeling the greatest. I think I'm going to have my meals delivered, and rest up for a few days."

"Sorry, you're not feeling well," Gert, said. "A little rest can't hurt. We'll check back in a day or two. Let us know if you need anything."

"Thanks," Nora replied. The fear was still in her eyes as she closed the door.

Gertrude and I continued on to breakfast.

"This is an inside job. It has to be. No one could bug her place, move things and place the flower pot in front of her door, unless it was someone that didn't look out of place."

"Sure looks that way," Gert agreed. "I was hoping it wasn't. This is frightening."

We walked through the door, and toward the comforting smell of cinnamon buns.

"Maybe I shouldn't have told you all that stuff in my place this morning. We might be bugged too. I'll call Det. Lancaster when we get outside. I want to see if he found out anything about Eddie's brother. I was so involved with Nora's problem, it slipped my mind."

"Speaking of Nora," Gert said, "I can't help but feel sorry for her and bad about how we tried to avoid her, but she was very foolish to act as she did, just because she was poor. Most of us were poor when we were kids. I remember having only two dresses in high school, and wearing one every other day. Didn't hurt me any. She just got off track somewhere. Too bad. She could've had a much happier life. I only hope her husband loved and understood her."

"I agree."

We ate our meal, and left the building.

"How about we walk while I call Detective Lancaster? Better not to take any chances until we know for sure if there are bugs in our places."

"Yes. That would probably be best."

The detective answered on the first ring.

"Just picked up my phone to call you," he said.

"Great. Last night I forgot to ask you about Eddie's family."

"I found out this morning, he had one brother, but he died two years ago. He lived in Kansas City. Neal was Eddie's only sibling. He doesn't seem to have any other living family: cousins, aunts, uncles, nothing. He must not have meant his brother, or was trying to say something else."

"Rats! I was hoping that would lead to something. I'll visit Eddie today and see if he can tell me anything more. Also, Gert and I are a little nervous now about our places being bugged. Can you help us find out if we're safe to talk in our homes?"

"Sure, we can do that. What cable company do you use for your TV?"

"Dish Network."

"A serviceman will call on each of you. Seems you both decided to add HBO," he said with a chuckle. "It may be tomorrow before I can get it arranged. You do pay for your own cable, don't you?"

"Yes."

"Good. People shouldn't ask questions then."

"We appreciate it. We'll find other places to talk until you get our cabins checked. I'll let you know if Eddie tells me anything today. Thanks again."

I hung up, silently thanked the Lord for cell phones, and we sat on a nearby bench. A cool breeze fluffed the leaves on a small branch beside us.

"Morning, ladies."

Oh, damn it to hell! It was Big Jim again. That man is like a zombie; no sound seems to come from those enormous feet. Had he heard my conversation with Det. Lancaster?

"Good morning," I said, with a bit of hesitation. Gert spoke in a more normal manner. He didn't seem to spook her like he did me, but she hadn't seen him staring at us through the fence. I had to check him out, some more, even if he was huge and intimidating. He ambled away as quietly as he had arrived.

"Do you want to go with me to the hospital?" I asked Gert, trying to return to a sane state of mind. "I'll park closer this time."

"Yes, I want to know how he's doing, and if he says anything. My feet are still sore, but we can wear our tennis shoes. I'm sure Eddie won't mind. I told you I would help with this mess, and I meant it. Also, we can discuss things in the car that we can't say here."

"Right oh." I said, giving her a pat on the back.

We stood, dusted off our bottoms and agreed to change shoes and meet there in ten minutes.

With shoes changed, we met again at the bench. I saw Gert's look of disapproval as she glanced at my frilly, lace socks and tennis shoes, but she didn't comment. Hell, I didn't have any other clean socks. This time I didn't have a choice. I made a mental note to send my laundry to be done when I got back. Too damn much stuff going on. I was running behind on my household chores, not that that didn't happen now and then, but geez.

Hot damn! A car was pulling out of the front row. I had my little red baby in that space before anyone else could get a foot near his gas pedal. Dang, I hoped this was a sign the rest of the day would go as well.

It was a gorgeous day. The temperature was perfect. The flags in front of the hospital waved lazily, caressed by a flower-scented breeze. How could anything go wrong on a day like this?

We entered the hospital. Gert pulled out her Word Search book and headed to the coffee shop. I headed for the fifth floor.

"Your name please?" asked a young officer when I arrived.

He was a different one than before.

"Joyce Greenly," I said, handing over my driver's license.

He looked at his clipboard and said, "Thank you. You can go in, but I understand he's had a pretty rough day. He may not know you're here."

I went to Eddie's bedside, hoping the young man was wrong.

"Hello, Eddie, it's Joyce." I said to a man who looked like a tree limb from the aftermath of a tornado. The machine over his head was making the usual beeps and squiggly lines. Not truly trusting it, I placed my hand on his chest and felt his heart beating. He was alive, but would he ever talk to me again?

"Listen to me, Eddie. Don't you dare die on me. I need you to help me catch the evil person who did this to you. You hear me?" My mouth was practically on his ear. His body gave no sign that my words had made it to his brain.

I patted his chest gently, and left his side feeling sad and deflated. With my head down, and walking toward the door, I ran smack into someone. As we untangled ourselves and I looked up, it was obvious he was probably a physician.

"Oh, I'm so sorry. Are you Eddie's doctor?"

"One of them," he said, rearranging his stethoscope. "Are you a relative?"

"No, he doesn't have any. I'm a friend." Again, the ugly things I'd said about Eddie a few days ago flitted through my brain. How's he doing? He doesn't seem very well today."

"He's not ready to run any races, but he's not as bad as he looks. He developed an infection, and one of the antibiotics didn't set well. He was also in a lot of pain, so it's probably the pain meds that have him out of it. I expect he'll be better in a couple of days."

"That's good to hear," I said, still feeling a little unsure. "Will he really be back to normal? Is he going to make it?"

"I try not to make promises I don't have total control over, but I think he'll recover. It will take a lot of hard work. As you can see, he has several broken bones and a head injury. It's going to be awhile, and we have to get this infection under control. Don't worry," he said, patting me on the shoulder. "We're taking good care of him. I shouldn't be telling you all this, but since you seem to be his only contact, I think it's important for patients to know someone cares."

"Thanks so much. I'll get out of your hair now, and let you check on him."

He nodded, and I left the room.

I couldn't shake my worries about Eddie, as I walked toward the elevator. Life had gone from higher than a kite, to lower than a snail in matter of minutes. A sudden burst of anger and hate hit me like a bolt of lightning. I'll be damned, if I let this get me down. If we can get our hands on the person who started all this, I'll rip their face off.

Back on the first floor, I entered the coffee shop. Gert had her head down, working on her word search. I went to the counter and ordered a latte. Drink in hand, I walked to Gert's table and plopped down.

She looked up and said, "I thought you'd be gone longer." She saw my face and said, "What's wrong?"

"We're going to catch that "shit-faced" killer!"

"What?" Gert said, in amazement. She quickly looked around the room to see if anyone else had heard my outburst; her face turning a rosy pink.

"Sorry, but I'm upset, to say the least. Eddie looked like the devil, and was out cold. One of his doctors came in. He thinks he will be okay, but I can't keep from worrying about him. What if he doesn't make it? How will we find the filthy creature who murdered Jake, broke Nora's leg, and pushed Eddie down the stairs?"

"Joyce, we'll find him! It's not like you to give up."

"Who the hell said I was giving up?" I replied, through my teeth. "You know me better than that," I snarled. We sat: me steaming and Gert looking like a mouse wanting the cheese, but afraid of the cat.

"Sorry," I said, sipping my latte. "It was so upsetting to see him in such bad shape. I was so ready to get a clue from Eddie, and when I saw him in that condition, it made me apprehensive and furious at the same time. Don't worry. I'll get back on track and think of something."

We finished our coffee and headed to the parking lot. It was still a beautiful day…until we got to the car.

"Oh, damn it to hell! I've got a flat," I said, as we approached my sweet ride. Keep your cool, Joyce, I told myself, taking deep breathes. As we came around the now lower corner of the car, we both sucked in a breath of disbelief. Sticking out of the tire was a wicked looking knife. We stared in disbelief.

"What in hell?" I gasped.

"Why would someone slash your tire, and why would they leave the knife behind?" asked Gert.

"To send a message," I said, looking around the huge lot. That was useless. The person who did this was probably long gone, and savoring their success.

"You think this has to do with Eddie?" Gert asked.

"Eddie, Jake and Nora too. Someone wants us to back off. This is Nora's flowerpot. He, they, whoever wants us to sit back and be 'little old ladies'.

"It's time to call Detective Lancaster."

Chapter 17

Within an hour and a half, the police had taken pictures, dusted the knife and car for prints, and asked the hospital about surveillance film. Maybe, since we were on the first row, the cameras might have caught something. AAA had changed my tire, and the Detective asked us to go home and lay low until he did some more checking and got back with us. We headed home, not knowing if we were running away from, or toward danger.

"Gert, you still have your laptop don't you?"

"Yes, why?"

"I was just wondering if it would do any good to do some research on Neal Thompson, Eddie's brother."

"Why? What would we look for?"

"I don't know, but it's about all we have to work with. Maybe it would help us find out more about Eddie. If we both work at the same time, one of us might come up with something the other missed. We can't ask the police for more help, so we'll just have to do it the hard way."

"Guess it's worth a try," Gert agreed. "Since we can't talk in our places until tomorrow, where are we going to work?"

"How about the Mud House. They have sandwiches, as well as coffee and Wi-Fi. They usually have a good crowd, so we could probably whisper without being heard. Our biggest problem is getting out of The White Dove without anyone seeing us. We don't want to be followed again."

"Maybe we need to try Nora's trick," Gert said.

"Oh, Gertrude, that's an excellent idea. Let's take a look in the Salvation Army store, and see if they have some things that might work."

After browsing through the thrift store, we walked out with a set of nurses' scrubs, sturdy shoes, a large yellow dress, God ugly orange high heels, some gaudy jewelry and a long brown wig to cover my red hair. We giggled like a couple of little girls at the thought of how we would look in the clothes; a stark contrast to the serious situation that held us hostage.

Back in the car, I said, "I'll change and leave first. Give me time to walk over to Price Cutter, and then pick me up in your car. We usually drive mine, so it's the one that would be noticed, but do look around carefully. If you see anyone, just call me and walk to meet me. If need be, we can call an Uber. That would mean we wouldn't be able to change in your car, so we would have to go to the Mud House in our getups," I said with a smile. It wouldn't bother me, but Gert was a little more sensitive about her looks. (Those words would bite me later.)

I waited a bit when we arrived at the White Dove, so Gert could make it to her cabin. We thought it would draw less attention if we went in separately with our large bags.

Now in my cabin, the huge yellow dress lay on my bed. It

would take some padding to make it fit. My thermal vest with a small throw pillow in the back of my panty hose worked beautifully. With the jewelry, wig and shoes in place, a different woman appeared. I didn't recognize my reflection in the mirror. It wasn't a flattering look, but the important thing was, it would take a close look to know who was under that conglomeration. I put on some big sunglasses and a scarf type shawl to cover my arms. They looked a little puny for my big butt. Now, the plan was to pass as a visitor leaving, after spending time with a friend.

I put my laptop and a dress in a black tote bag, and called Gert, but hung up after one ring. It was our pre-arranged signal to let her know the big lady in the yellow dress was heading out. I slipped through the back door, after checking to see if anyone was around; walked down two cabins and came out between the second and third. There was only one person in sight. She was walking the other way, and took no notice of me. Most residents were probably taking after lunch naps. Which reminded me, Gert and I hadn't had any lunch. We'd fix that. I was hungry.

Fifteen minutes later Gert pulled up beside me. "Oh, my gosh. I wouldn't have recognized you if it weren't for the yellow dress," she said, with a giggle.

"You sure don't look like yourself either."

Gert had also put on some fancy sunglasses; ones I'm sure had been left behind by her daughter, Janet. Gert didn't wear pink sparkles. She had wrapped her head in a scarf, which was tied in the back, covering all her grey hair. Her lips were bright red: again thanks to Janet.

My butt stuffing was too high to sit on. This made it difficult to sit back normally. I was trying to adjust when my phone rang. I grabbed my purse, dug quickly and came out with Mozart playing in my hand.

"Hello."

"Mrs. Greenly, this is Detective Lancaster. "Are you where you can talk?"

"Yes, we're in Gert's car."

"Good. I wanted to let you know the hospital security tape shows our guy. It didn't take long to find it, since we had a narrow time period. It shows a guy; at least we think it's a man, dressed in jeans, a denim shirt, and a large straw hat. He came in a cab, which he had stop just past your car. He got out, walked to the front fender, looked around, and bent toward your tire. He stood up, keeping his head down, and walked back to the cab. We checked with the cab company. The driver said he picked him up at the Battlefield Mall, and then took him back to the mall. The driver didn't see what he did to your car, but thought the whole thing was bizarre, and had already reported it to his supervisor. He said the person hardly said a word, other than, "Mercy Hospital, Battlefield Mall, and stop".

"Hell fire. Who are we dealing with? He must have

followed us to the hospital in his own car to know we had parked in the first row; otherwise his little plan wouldn't have worked. Shit! Oh sorry. I'm just a little rattled."

"As well you should be," offered Det. Lancaster. "I'm only telling you this so you will understand the situation. This person, or multiple people for all we know, is obviously dangerous. We've decided to move you to a safe house until we can have a look at your cabins. Where are you now?"

"Ahh," I stammered, as I contemplated our ridiculous clothing. The phone was on speaker, and Gert looked at me like a cat with his tail in the screen door. "Well, we are in Gert's car in Price Cutter's parking lot. We sneaked out in disguise," I said, thinking how much I didn't want HIM to see us like this.

"Clever," he chuckled. "We know your cars. I'll have a black SUV there in a few minutes. The last three digits of the license plate will be 549. He'll flash his lights to let you know it's him. Follow him, and he'll take you to the safe house. Pull in the garage to hide your car."

"But we don't have any clothes or PJ's," I stammered.

"There should be clothing of different sizes at the house; toothbrushes, shampoo and about anything you need. The garage door will open as you pull up, so you can drive inside. Any questions?"

Yes, I thought. How long does it take two older women to change clothes in a moving car?

"No," I answered.

"Good. I'll be by to talk with you in a bit. I also need to borrow your keys so our man can check your places for listening devices."

"Okay," I said, and hung up quickly.

"Damn, damn, double damn," I said. "We've got to get these clothes off." I looked over and realized Gert was already ahead of me. She had her scarf and glasses off and was working on the lipstick with a tissue.

Panicked, I yanked off my wig, and threw it in the back seat, along with the sunglasses. Pulling the dress up as far as it could go; I struggled to remove the pillow.

This was not going to be easy. I unfastened my seat belt and scooted toward the dash. Gert reached over and gave some yanks. After a prolonged effort, the pillow was tossed in the back, but now came the worst part. The dress had to be up around my neck, in order to unbutton the puffy vest. I had the obnoxious yellow cloth up under my arms, and one button unfastened on the vest, when the police car showed up. He flashed his lights, and proceeded through the lot, expecting us to fall in line.

"I've got to follow," Gert said, looking frantic.

"Yes, you do," I said, with the dress around my shoulders, my arms thrashing like a windmill; I wished the vest had a zipper. With my seatbelt off, it made it harder than hell to keep my balance. I bounced off the dash, the back of the seat, and my ribs took some rebounds off the door handle. A block later, thanks to a red light, I got the vest off, and added it to the pile. Now came the struggle to get the dress over my head. I'd had to put one arm back through the dress sleeve in order to get the vest off the other arm. I managed to get the dress partly up, but struggle as I might, the neck kept hanging on one side or the other and the fabric seemed glued to my sweaty back. I couldn't reach the two buttons at the back of the neck.

"Get your hand out of my face," Gert, yelled, giving my arm a good smack. "I can't see where I'm going," she scolded.

I hadn't realized I was getting in her space. "Sorry," I apologized. This just wasn't going to work in such a tight space, and besides, we were in double lane traffic. If I pulled the dress off over my head, we could pull up to a light, and some guy in his pickup truck, would have a clear view of me in my bra. Forget the dress in your bag, Joyce! My only hope was to get the other arm back in, and pull the yellow tent down when we got to the garage. Otherwise, the person greeting us would be treated to a view of my underpants.

"I can't take these scrubs off," said Gert. "I only have leggings and a t-shirt on under them. They are way too tight and revealing."

"Well, at least you're not stuck in a neon yellow dress the size of an awning, and hooker shoes," I growled. I was sweating like a pig, and in a pissy mood after my struggles in the restricted space.

"Calm down, Joyce. At least we're out of the White Dove, and headed to a place where we can relax for a bit, despite how we look."

"Yeah, I guess you're right," I said, begrudgingly. We drove a couple of blocks through a residential neighborhood when a thought dawned on me. "Maybe they'll have Wi-Fi," I said in a more hopeful tone. "We can do our research there. But first we need to order some take-out. I don't know about you, but I'm starving. It's 4:30 and we haven't had anything to eat since breakfast."

"Amen," Gert chimed in. "I could eat a mule."

Chapter 18

My mood was a bit brighter as the black SUV slowed and stopped in front of an ordinary looking house. Immediately the garage door went up. We were home.

"This must be it," Gert said, turning into the driveway and toward the garage.

It was an ordinary ranch style house, with low, well-tended flowerbeds, and a nice lawn.

The door going into the house from the garage opened a bit as Gert pulled inside. I was relieved to see a female peeking out at us. At least it would be a woman seeing my underpants. The garage door started down as soon as Gert's taillights cleared. I opened the car door, and scooted along the seat, tugging at my dress tail to follow, and struggling to get my left hand back in the sleeve. I was thankful to be on the far side of the car. I could now stand up and redress myself in relative privacy.

"Hello, ladies. Welcome to your temporary home," the young officer said. "Come on in. I understand you were pretty much snatched off the street, and don't have anything with you. Let me show you around, and you can help yourselves to anything you need."

"Thanks," we said in unison, like a couple of sweating parrots.

"Do you have Wi-Fi?" I asked right off the bat. "We'll bring our laptops in, if you do."

"We do. It comes in handy. We use it quite often."

Gert and I smiled, and grabbed our laptop bags and purses, which were all we had to move into our new home.

The house was furnished in a pale blue, grey and white theme. There was a comfortable looking recliner close to the front door. Probably a popular and necessary spot for whoever might be guarding the place. A matching sofa, armchair, two end tables and a coffee table completed the living room area, except for a dining table in the corner near the kitchen. All in all it was a warm cozy looking space: one where people like us wouldn't mind spending some time.

"I'm Officer Gail Pence. Just call me Gail." She was dressed in a nice black suit, comfortable shoes, and was about five foot seven, with short brown hair.

Since we were dealing with another female, we felt more comfortable as we explained our wonky clothing. Thankfully, she didn't laugh. She'd probably seen all sorts of things.

"There are clothes in the closet and drawers in the master bedroom. You might find something more comfortable. Hopefully there will be some suitable shoes, if you'd like to get out of those heals," she said, with a glance at my feet.

"We appreciate all your help. There's just one more thing, if you don't mind. We haven't had any food since breakfast. Could we order a pizza, sandwiches or something?" I asked.

"Sure, give me your order."

Food choices given, Gert and I made our way into the bedroom the officer pointed out.

"Holy hell!" I gasped, as I passed a mirror and saw my reflection. "Gert! Why didn't you tell me I look like a "psycho rooster"? I scolded.

Gert stared at me in obvious shock. "Joyce, I'm, I'm so sorry. I haven't even looked at you since we got out of the car." Although she was trying to hide it, I could see her desperately trying to stifle a grin and a giggle, in the wake of my wrath.

Staring back from the mirror was a creature with spiked red hair sticking in all directions. My bright red lipstick had made a couple of smeared crimson streaks toward my eyebrows, and the JEWELRY! I still had on the hideous, bulky, gaudy jewelry. Why didn't I get rid of that? I should have taken it off first. It would have helped not to have it in the way. In my effort to yank the wig off, pull the dress up around my neck, rid myself of the puffy vest, and worry about my underpants showing, I had created a wild eyed creature never before seen by man. I'd had my normal dress in my computer bag. Fat lot of good that did. Since I was unable to get the yellow one off in time, it now showcased the rest of the jumble. Only, without the pillow and vest, it was hanging on me like a deflated balloon. Oh, and of course, my 'hooker shoes.' They set off the rest of the glorious picture.

I dug in my purse, grabbed my comb, and tried to destroy the rooster.

"Oh, my gosh! I can't believe I was out there carrying on, what I thought was a serious conversation, with that lady officer, and all the time I was looking like a freak show," I said, struggling between yelling, anger and pouting. Gert may not always approve of my attire, but I do try hard to look my best, and this wasn't it.

Gert evidently decided that, in my present state, I should probably be left alone. She turned to the closet and was looking for a dress or some more modestly loose clothing.

I removed the yellow dress, lipstick, colorful streaks, and jewelry. I pulled my now wrinkled dress out of my bag. Put it on and found some flat black shoes, somewhere between loafers and tennis shoes, in the closet. I was almost afraid to look, but at least the mirror didn't shriek at me this time.

Just as we finished putting ourselves together, we heard the doorbell. I hoped it was our food. Instead, I heard Det. Lancaster's voice.

Seconds later, the female officer knocked on the bedroom door. "Are you ladies finished dressing?" she asked.

Gert opened the door, and we were thrilled to see the detective, now in plain clothing, holding a Jimmy Johns bag.

"Dinner, ladies?" he said, with a big grin.

"Oh, man, are we glad to see some food?" I said, practically slobbering over the thought of the warm, juicy sandwiches inside.

He set the bag on the dining table and motioned for us to have a seat.

"Water, soda or coffee?" asked Officer Gail.

"Diet Coke, if you have it," I answered.

"Water for me," Gert, chimed in.

Gail headed to the kitchen to get our drinks.

"Thank you, Det. Lancaster. We were famished."

"You're welcome. I was headed this way, and we try to pick-up food ourselves if possible. That way we don't draw as much attention to the house. If we're in plain clothes, the delivery people don't suspect anything, and we try to vary our food orders, so the neighbors don't think the tenants here are hooked on Dominoes. We decided I would get it since I was coming anyway. I'll shut up for a bit, and let you enjoy your food," he said, with a grin.

Officer Gail picked up another Jimmy John's bag I hadn't noticed, and headed back to the kitchen to eat hers in peace and quiet, or maybe peruse Facebook, I don't know.

We dived into our sandwiches, like starving wolves. The warm melting cheese almost made me weep.

As we finished the last potato chip crumbs, and sipped our drinks, Det. Lancaster, who'd been on his phone, returned to the table and sat down.

"We went over the security tape from the mall. The taxi driver told us he dropped the suspect off at the food court.

That is, of course, the busiest entrance to the mall: people wanting food, the "walkers" come in that way, and one of the bathrooms is there. We finally picked him out of the crowd. He bought a drink at Taco Bell, sat and leisurely drank it, threw the cup in the trash, and walked to the bathroom. After that, we didn't see him again. I'm sure we did, but we didn't recognize him. No one came out that looked anything like him. We have people going through the trash to see if we can locate the hat he was wearing when he went in. If we can find it, we might get some DNA to help track him down, if he's in the system…big 'if'. The Taco Bell cup would be by far the best, but there are too many of those."

He sighed and continued, "There are too many ways to go in and out of the mall to have a chance of picking him out. He most likely had a vehicle parked near one of the exits, but since we have no idea what he looked like when he left, it would be impossible to pick him out. Hell, he might have looked like a female when he left. Both the men and women's restrooms are down that hall. He could even have had an accomplice waiting with a disguise. Very frustrating. I want this guy bad."

The Detective looked up as if coming out of a trance. I think he had been so involved with the case, he had forgotten everything but the madding information twirling through his head.

"Sorry, didn't mean to go on like that, but guess I brought

you up to date," he said, with a sheepish grin. "I shouldn't be telling you all this information. I'd appreciate it if you didn't spread it around. I seem to be making a habit of treating you as official officers. I need to watch that."

"Glad you trust us," I chimed in. "Your idea about there being more than one person has crossed our minds, too. He seems to cover a lot of territory. We also thought it would have been difficult for one person to have gotten Jake from his cabin to the gazebo, and why wasn't he just left in his cabin?"

"Good questions. They bug me too. Should have known you'd pick up on them too," he said. "Now, for the present, we still need you to try and find out if Eddie can tell you anything. I understand you weren't able to talk to him today, but we still need you to try. Perhaps it would be better not to go tomorrow. He could probably use some time to recover a bit from the infection. When you go again, take an Uber and enter through the North Emergency Room door. There are elevators there that will take you part way. You may have to ask for directions, and change elevators. It's rather confusing. Some don't go all the way to the fifth floor, but one of them should bring you out closer to Eddie's room than if you came in the front door. Hopefully, no one will expect you to come in the back. Most people don't."

"Mrs. Bush, you may want to have the driver stop at Starbucks on the way. You'll most likely have to sit in the Emergency waiting room. They are kind of short on good coffee," he said, with a smile.

"How long are we going to be here?" Gertrude asked, looking around the room.

"Hopefully, not too long. You said you didn't check out when you left the White Dove?"

"No. We left in disguise, so no one knows we're gone," I answered. "Someone might miss us at breakfast, but we do sometimes go out for brunch. So, we should be okay for a while."

"Good. We want to have time to get our tech person in your places to see if anything is there that shouldn't be. I've already heard from the agent in regard to Mrs. Woolworth's place. She found no evidence the place was bugged. She thinks someone is just moving things around to scare her, so she'll stop asking questions. I hope it will be the same in your cottages. Since they know you're in contact with us, they have probably thought it a bit risky to enter your space."

"So does that mean we can go back tomorrow, if they don't find anything?" questioned Gert.

I know her well, and knew she was not as worried about staying here as she was about having her own clothes and underwear.

"Ordinarily, I would say yes, but I would feel better if you stayed here until we see if Eddie can tell us something. I don't want a repeat of the knife in the tire incident. We're planning to have a plain car follow you to the hospital and make sure no one tries to cause any trouble."

I could see the disappointment in Gert's face.

"Would it be possible for the person who checks our places to bring us some underwear and our PJ's?" I asked.

"Sure. I'll give him a call."

Gert's face lit up with concern. I knew it was the word, "him" that put it there. The thought of a man digging through her panties was appalling, I'm sure. Well, hell, you can't have it both ways. I tried.

"Oh, don't bother," Gert piped up. "We're not too far from Walmart. I could use some new things anyway. How about you Joyce?"

Well, damn! What could I say? I wanted to get started on researching Eddie and his brother. "Sounds fine to me."

"That's okay, but I'd rather you take an Uber instead of your car. Just in case our guy might recognize yours. Officer Pence will need to go with you. We don't want to take any chances.

"By the way, Deputy Brighton said to tell you, "Hi. He appreciates your help, and to be careful. He had to go back east for a bit."

"I'd better be going, but I'll run by again tomorrow: see how you're doing and if you need anything. You should make your trip to Walmart soon. Officer Pence will be off duty in a little over an hour. Oh, and I need to borrow your keys to let our tech guy in."

We got our keys from our purses, and handed them over.

He opened the door, said "Thanks, see you tomorrow," and was gone.

Chapter 19

"Ladies," Officer Gail spoke up, "I probably shouldn't follow you around like we're a threesome. I'll say I need to get some cookies, and have the driver let me off on the grocery end of the store. You ask him to take you to the other door, because it is closer to what you need. I'll watch for you to come in, and keep a close eye on you, but will keep my distance. I'm going to have my replacement pick us up in a plain car. Let me take a quick pic of the two of you, so he'll know who to pick-up.

We posed, and she pushed the camera button on her phone.

She stood for a few minutes, and appeared to be texting the other officer.

"Okay, it's all set. The car will have a "Prime Realty" sticker on it, so you can be sure it's him. Get in the back seat. I won't be far behind, and will get in the front. This may sound a little much, but I'd rather not have another Uber driver seeing us together. Even if I'm not in uniform, these suits are a bit too familiar, especially to criminals. Now, let me call an Uber and we'll be on our way," she said, with an all business look.

Gert and I headed to the bedroom to grab our purses and apply some lipstick. I was glad Officer Gail was taking our welfare seriously, but it also put me in a tense mood. The last few days had been filled with horror, suspense, and mistrust. I had been running on adrenalin, with little time to rest and collect my thoughts. Now, all that was visible in my head was Jake's body, with the hateful knife protruding from his back. Suddenly, the vision jumped to the knife jammed in my tire. This guy likes knives; I don't like knives. A shiver rolled down my spine.

I looked at Gertrude's tense expression, and suspected she might not be in a happy place either. Hopefully I was wrong. This wasn't her deal. It was, though I'd rather not admit it, a bit intense for me. But, I'd be damned if I give up.

"Are you ready?" asked Gert.

I took a quick peek in the mirror, to avoid another rooster event, and nodded, "Yes."

The time it took our ride to arrive was impressive. Dang, that was service. We had arranged for Officer Pence to sit behind the driver. He would not have the view of her he had of us. I sat in the front seat. We would have to distract him when she got out at the store. He probably wouldn't even realize she was an officer, but just in case, since she thought it would be to our advantage, we'd do our best.

The car pulled up to the grocery entrance, and Officer Pence made a quick exit. Before her feet hit the pavement, I turned my coin purse upside down in the front passenger floorboard.

"Oh, my goodness," I exclaimed. "I'm so sorry. Do you

mind pulling closer to the other entrance? The light's better there. I'm going to have to get out to gather this up. I'll have to look under the seat. I don't want to miss anything. My mother's ring was in there."

He didn't look particularly happy, but was courteous, and did as he was asked. He even handed me a small flashlight. It didn't take long to gather the spilled coins, and the driver got a little extra for his trouble.

When we got out of the Uber, the door to the store's grocery section was visible. Officer Gail was watching our progress from inside the glass. Mission accomplished.

As we walked inside, I wondered if Gert was thinking what I was. Shopping at Dillard or Macy's for new undies would have been more satisfying, but since they were located in the mall, and the assumed killer evidently knew the place well, this would have to do. The mall was off limits until this was over. I was gloomy again, and Gertrude didn't look any better as we headed for "Women's Wear."

We gathered a few necessary items. The best underwear doesn't come in plastic bags of six, but this wasn't the time to be picky. We each found panties, a suitable pair of pajamas and a light robe. Officer Pence was browsing through socks, a couple of aisles over; her eyes flitting toward us every few minutes. We completed our shopping, and headed for the checkout lanes. Our guard followed a discrete distance behind.

Knowing how weak we humans are, the stores always have

an array of goodies to admire while you're waiting in line. I couldn't resist a small package of Ruffles, a bag of cheese curls and a Payday bar. Dang it! However, my guilt subsided a bit when Gert picked up a package of cashews, and a Hershey bar. No will power for either of us, but then we didn't know what was on the shelves of our hideout home: my excuse anyway.

As planned, the car was waiting just outside the door, in the pickup lane. The officer motioned for us to get in the back.

"Hello ladies," he said, and then proceeded down Row 7, stopped, and Officer Pence, who stood between an SUV and a van, hopped in the front seat.

"Hi, Roger. Ladies, this is Officer Roger Millsap. Roger, this is Mrs. Greenly and Mrs. Bush," she said, pointing to each of us respectively.

A short time later, we pulled into the driveway of our hideout. It should have taken about half the time, but it was evident that Officer Millsap was taking the long way in an effort to make sure we were not being followed.

Officer Pence, said goodnight, and added she would probably see us tomorrow afternoon. We watched her walk to a car we hadn't noticed before. It was parked in a space between some tall bushes, and was hardly visible. She got in and disappeared into the night.

When we entered the house, Roger, as he had told us to call him, announced that Domino's would be delivering a couple of pizzas in thirty minutes.

"Are you hungry?"

"I could go for a couple of slices," I answered, even though it hadn't been all that long since we gobbled down the Jimmy John's feast. Of course, he didn't know that, and was trying to be thoughtful by offering us dinner.

Gert nodded in agreement.

"While we're waiting, could you give us the Wi-Fi password? We have our laptops with us and would like to catch-up on some things."

"Sure," he answered. "There's a printer in the linen closet if you need it. Let me get you setup and I'll call you when the pizza's here."

"Man, I can't believe we are finally getting to do this," I said to Gert, after Roger had closed the bedroom door.

"Me either. This is a long way from the Mud House, but we're finally hooked up," she said, sitting at a small desk.

I was propped up on some pillows against the headboard.

"You want to Google about Eddie, and I'll try his brother, Neal. Neal was supposed to be in the Kansas City area, but I'm not sure about Eddie."

"I'll try KC first. If I don't get anything, I'll try a broader search," Gert answered.

For the time being, we wanted to keep our efforts quiet, just in case we didn't turn up anything. Besides, if we did find something, we wanted to rub Agent Niger's nose in it.

We had hardly gotten started when the pizza arrived.

"Damn it!"

We pretty much had to eat at the table. Roger would wonder what was so important that we had to browse our computers instead of eating like civilized humans. We couldn't put our greasy paws on our laptops without some explanation. So to the table we went.

We ate in record time; cleaned up the crumbs and soda can circles on the table and drifted toward our room. I hoped Officer Roger didn't think we were rude. I yawned several times to suggest we were tired. That wasn't much of a stretch.

Back at my computer, I pulled up Google, typed in "Neal Thompson, Kansas City" and before I could hit "return," Mozart began to play beside me.

"Hello."

"Joyce this is Nora. I wanted to thank you, and also see if you're okay. I haven't seen you all day."

Oh, geesh. I don't like lying to people, especially not to someone I now considered a friend. I would just have to rearrange the truth a bit: no way around it.

"I'm fine," I said. Gert and I had Jimmy Johns instead of going to the dining room. We're just a bit tired, and decided to take it easy this evening. We may not get out much tomorrow either. We've just had so much going on, as have you. We thought it would be nice to relax and catch up on some reading for a day or two. I'm also running ideas through my head to see who could be at the bottom of all this."

"Oh, Joyce, I'm sorry I added to your stress, but I want to thank you so much for your help in getting my place checked out. It is wonderful to be able to talk on the phone, and since I'm staying in, I no longer have things moving around in my place. I won't keep you, but it's so nice to have you as a friend now. You get some rest, and I'll talk to you soon."

"You are welcome, and you take it easy, too."

We hung up. It was good to see this side of Nora, but I still felt guilty about things I'd said about her in the past, and what she'd gone through that spurred her to make the change.

I repeated Nora's side of the conversation to Gert, and hit "return."

About sixteen "Neal Thompsons popped up in the Kansas City area. Oh, hell. This was going to take some time to sort out. After attempting to weed out the ones less than forty years old, I hit upon the idea of looking for "Neal Thompson Obituary." Bingo. It went down to five.

Neal Edward Thompson-1918—1996. Nope: too long ago.

Judge Neal Joseph Thompson-1950—2015. I stared at this one for a few minutes, before I was able to believe this could actually be the one. I read the list of survivors and my heart did a flip as I read: 'Edward Gene Thompson of Chesterfield, MO - brother.'

"Gert," I yelled, almost dumping my laptop in the floor. "I found him, I found him!"

Gertrude jumped, and stared at me like I had hit her with a bat. She had been so engrossed in what she was doing; she just stared at me for a few seconds, until what I said found a place in her brain.

"You did? What did you find?"

"His obituary. Eddie is listed, and it says he's from Chesterfield, MO. That's a suburb of St. Louis. Now, at least, you know where to look for him."

"Finally; a straw. I was wandering around coming up with nothing. This'll narrow it down. What are you going to do next?"

"I'm going to call the Chesterfield Police to see if anyone there knows him or if they know anyone who might. Think I'll wait until tomorrow though. I don't know about you, but this day just caught up with me. Add the pizza, and I can hardly keep my eyes open."

"I agree completely. I'm ready for my PJ's and some down time. How about we get ready for bed and see if there's something funny on TV. I could use some 'funny'."

It didn't take long for us to change clothes, brush our teeth and plop on the large bed, close to the TV. The room was good sized. It had a full and a twin bed.

Gert had already put her things on the small bed. I suggested we trade, but she said, 'No', so we left it as it was. We failed to find the 'funny' Gert was looking for, but settled on 'First Time Flippers' on DIY. Within thirty minutes, we had both slid to a horizontal position and were straining to keep our eyes open. We turned off the TV and got in our respective beds. Lights out.

Chapter 20

Morning came with the usual "Where am I?" moment. I love to travel, stay in motels and hotels, but this was like sleeping in someone else's home: a stranger's home. I wanted MY home. I wondered when in hell that would happen. Today? Tomorrow? It couldn't come soon enough.

A tiny shred of sunshine had made it through the heavy blinds and fell across Gert's shoulder. Somehow it reminded me of how vulnerable my dearest friend in the world was. I had to get her safely through this: had to.

Gert stirred, and I saw the flicker of confusion in her eyes.

"Good morning, my friend. You want the shower first?" I asked, in a cheerful tone, hoping my smile reached my eyes.

"Good morning. No you go ahead. I think I'll stay under the covers for a bit."

"Okay, it won't take me long." I took a quick look in the closet, and decided the dress I'd brought with me might not be entirely clean, but it was my style and it fit. I headed to the shower thinking next time I cleaned my closet I'd donate a few things to this place.

It is amazing how much being squeaky clean and dressed can improve your attitude.

When I walked back into the bedroom, the smell of fresh coffee was floating under the door. It made the day seem even more appealing.

"You go get some of that coffee," Gert suggested. "I'll be out in a few minutes."

"I can wait."

"No. You go ahead. I'll hurry, and that smells too good to resist," she ordered.

"Okay. Wonder what they have to go with the coffee. I'm hungry," I said, with my hand on the doorknob, and curious who was behind it this morning.

"Good Morning. Are you Mrs. Greenly or Mrs. Bush?" asked a handsome young man as I entered the living room. He was sitting at the table with his phone in one hand, and a cup in the other.

"Mrs. Greenly, but call me Joyce."

"Jeremy Flynn here, Joyce. Are you ready for some coffee and a blueberry scone? We have some frozen sausage and egg biscuits if you would rather have savory. I might add though, the scones are fresh from the bakery."

"The scones sound wonderful. I'd love one. I'll help myself," I replied, as I turned toward the kitchen and the wonderful coffee smell.

Jeremy poured coffee while I put a fat, flakey scone on a paper plate.

"Would you like one, too?" I asked.

"Thanks, but I've already had two. They were still warm when they arrived, and it was rude, but I just couldn't wait," he said, with a sheepish grin.

"Oh, don't worry about that. I would have done the same," I said, pouring sugar and cream into my coffee. "I'm not waiting on Gertrude either."

We took our things back to the table in the other room; the kitchen only had a small bar. We sat down.

"You don't look old enough to be a police officer," I said, hoping that wasn't an insult.

Everyone looks younger as you age.

Jeremy laughed, and said, "I assure you I am old enough, but I am pretty new at it. This is the start of my second year. We newbies get the early morning shift on something like this. The bad guys are not usually early risers."

"I'm sure you know what you're doing," I added, in case he had taken my comment the wrong way.

"Detective Lancaster called and said to tell you he has someone going to your places this morning to check for listening devices. He said it might be okay for you to go home if they come up clean. He wants to talk to you though. The knife incident has him concerned."

"Yes, I don't like that either, but we would still like to go home as soon as we can."

I took a big bite of the wonderful scone, followed by a very satisfying sip of coffee.

"Detective Lancaster wants you to wait until after lunch to go to the hospital. He has several things going this morning, and he wants to be available in case there are any problems. He'd like you to call him after your visit, and let him know about Eddie."

Well, Hell! I wanted things to move faster, but thought, guess we can do some more research this morning, and make the call put on hold from last night.

We chatted as we sipped our coffee. Jeremy was a very nice and intelligent young man to be cooped up with. He made me wish I were a little younger, I thought sheepishly.

The bedroom door opened, and Gert came in looking fresh as a daisy.

"Good morning. You must be Mrs. Bush. I'm Jeremy Flynn. It's nice to meet you."

"Nice to meet you too."

"Sit down, Gert. I'll get you a scone and coffee," I said, heading to the kitchen.

While Gert had her breakfast, we gave her an update.

"I'd like to go home today, if possible," she said, echoing my previous words

"I understand. Most people feel the same, but it's important to keep you as safe as possible. Detective Lancaster and others, are working hard to clean up this case, and get you both back in your homes."

"Oh, I know. Gert and I will have to suck-it-up. We have some computer work to do. Maybe that will make the day go faster."

"We should get back to that," Gert replied. We rose, and headed to our room.

"There are movies in the dresser, if you need some entertainment," Jeremy offered.

"Thank you," we said, and closed our door.

"Are you going to call the Chesterfield police?" Gert asked.

"Right this minute."

I sat on the bed, and retrieved the number from my purse.

The phone rang twice. "Chesterfield Police Department. Officer Cain speaking."

"My name is Joyce Greenly. I'm a friend of Eddie Thompson. Eddie has been injured and I'm trying to track down friends or relatives to let them know. He is in serious condition, and we feel they would like to know. He's from Chesterfield, that's why I called you. It's a long shot, but do you or anyone else there know him?"

"I'm sorry. The name doesn't sound familiar, and we're a pretty good-sized city. I'll do some checking though. Can you tell me how old he is, or what he does for a living?"

"I don't know for sure, but I'd say he is around seventy, and he is retired. I don't know what he did before."

"I'll do what I can. That's not a lot to go on, but I'll pass the word around and see if someone might have heard of him. Give me your number and I'll call you back if something turns up."

After giving my number, we hung up. Gert was watching

me with questions in her eyes.

"The person who answered the phone doesn't know him, but he's going to do some checking, and pass the word around to see if anyone else might."

"Maybe we'll get lucky. Sure hope so. I'm going to call Janet. Can't let her know what's going on, but hearing her voice would be nice. I'll go in the bathroom, so if you get a call, she won't hear you." She grabbed her phone and closed the door behind her.

Left to my own devices, my head was spinning: where do we go from here? What thread do we pull next? Were there any threads to pull? Who the hell was the "knife" guy and how did he know we were at the hospital?

Mozart began playing. I wasn't expecting it. I jumped, and my phone fell to the floor. I snatched it up. "Hello."

"Is this Joyce Greenly?" a strange man asked.

"Yes, who is this?"

"This is Det. Goodwin from the Chesterfield Police Department. Is Eddie okay?"

"He's hanging in there. He's not in the greatest condition. He hasn't been able to talk yet. So, you know him?"

"Yes, I haven't seen him in quite a while; did talk to him not too long ago. I met Eddie through my brother. When he found out I was with the police department, he stuck to me like glue. I guess you know he was a private eye. Most tenacious guy ever."

"No. I thought perhaps he might have been. He didn't talk about it. But he did ask a lot of questions."

"I bet," Det. Goodwin remarked, with a chuckle. "He about drove me nuts over the Tony Rossi case. He was obsessed with it. Not sure why. It took place in Delaware. I couldn't help him much. I could share some of the public facts, but I understand it isn't completely tied up yet, so couldn't share everything. He never said whom he was working for, or if it was just a bee in his bonnet. Next thing I knew, he retired, or at least partially. He called about a week ago. I'm ashamed I didn't get in a big hurry to call him back. You think he's going to be okay?"

"The doctors think so, but Eddie's a mass of bandages, and unable to tell us much."

"What happened?"

I filled him in. We chatted a bit and he gave me his direct number, with orders to have Eddie call him when he was able.

Gertrude entered the room looking much more collected than when she went in to make her call. Janet was a "happy pill" for her mom.

I smiled at my best friend, relieved to see her cheerful.

"I found someone who knows Eddie."

"You did? How?" She plopped on the other side of the bed, looking excited.

"A Det. from Chesterfield heard someone was asking about Eddie, and called to see about him. He said Eddie was a retired

P.I. and had called him recently. He hadn't had time to call him back, but said Eddie was obsessed with a Tony Rossi case that took place in Delaware. He doesn't know why, as it was so far away."

"That doesn't make sense," Gert replied. "Why would he care about something that wasn't near his home, or at least in Missouri or Illinois? There must be more to the story."

"I don't know, but since we have some time to kill, you want to see what we can find on it?

"Sure. Anything we can do that might help us get home faster is fine with me."

"I'll run get us a couple of diet cokes before we start." I headed to the kitchen, and got two frosty cans of soda. Jeremy was on his phone, so we just nodded as I passed by.

Gert took the soda I handed her. She had her laptop on the desk, and was already working. I retrieved mine from the floor where it had been charging, opened the curtains, and let the morning sunshine lift our spirits.

Chapter 21

We had been Googling "Tony Rossi" for about thirty minutes, when Gert hissed softly, "Joyce look at this picture!"

With my face practically on her computer screen, I couldn't believe my eyes. Staring back at us were two beady little eyes on a snake pin!

"Gertrude, I could kiss you."

"I'll pass on that, but this is amazing. Here is our connection, is it not?"

"It sure as hell looks like it. Whose picture is that?"

Gert moved her cursor so we could read the caption: "*First day in court for Tony Rossi. Rossi is charged with drug smuggling, money laundering and murder. Eyewitness accounts from an unknown source will be admitted into evidence. The police have not yet released the identity of the witness.*" The article was from two years ago.

"Hot Damn, Gert. Hit print! This is big stuff. Rossi can't be our killer. He's in prison. But someone close to him sure as hell could be: a person who knows him well, or a relative. That pin is too much of a coincidence."

"Wonder why Eddie was interested in the case?"

"Don't know, but damn it, I hope he can tell me something today." I ran out to the linen closet and grabbed the picture off the printer. Our protector glanced up as I zipped into the closet, and ran back into the bedroom. He probably thought I was overly excited about an email I'd received or a sale ad from my favorite store. I didn't care.

"Let's see if we can find more pictures of the trial, or stories leading up to it, and afterward. Maybe we can get more info on who the eyewitness was. I have a bad feeling we already know. I'd love to talk to Deputy Brighton. Don't know if he would be allowed to tell us anything, but my pride is yelling, "Don't ask for help!" I want Niger to see us find answers on our own."

"Amen," replied Gert. She really had a bur under her saddle for the FBI Agent.

My head was spinning as I Googled info on Tony Rossi. Should we or shouldn't we tell Det. Lancaster what we had found? He had been so good to us, and was trying to keep us safe…still, I had only promised to tell him what Eddie said. This was a slippery slope, but dang. Gert and I both had a score to settle with Niger; or at least, we felt we did.

Pushing my guilt aside, I searched for the name Rossi in Wilmington, DE. It's not a huge city, so my results were limited. Anthony, Anthony Jr., Gary, Helen and Carlo popped up.

Just because the trial was there didn't prove that these people were related to him, but from my experience, people involved in these types of crimes seem to be a tight-knit group. If the trial hadn't had a change of venue, Wilmington was certainly worth looking into.

Gary and Carlo didn't tell me much, so next was Helen. She seemed to be a more social person: active in "Wee-child" a children's charity, and past president of Roses in Bloom. More searching turned up a mention of her and her husband, Anthony, Sr., donating money for a monkey exhibit. I was overjoyed as the article mentioned their son, Tony Jr. and his older brother Henry's love of monkeys as the reason for their gift.

"Gert, I think I've found Tony Rossi's family! See if you can find anything on Helen, Anthony or Henry Rossi."

She grabbed a pen, jotted down the names, and set to work again. Two hours later, we had printed several articles mentioning the good and the bad of the Rossi family. The family had apparently been prominent, and successful, although Anthony Sr., an investment banker, was involved in some questionable real estate deals. He died of a heart attack in 1995, and Tony took over the business. We knew how that turned out.

"You ladies ready to order lunch?" Officer Flynn called through the door.

"Sure," I answered. My back and neck were complaining about how long I'd been hunched over my laptop, although we were on such a roll, it was hard to stop.

"Oh, man," Gertrude said, stretching her arms toward the ceiling. "I didn't realize how stiff I was until I tried to move.

My neck needs a break."

We stretched, and waddled toward the living room. We entered the room as Det. Lancaster came through the front door. It was difficult to read his facial expression; was he pleased or concerned?

"Hello ladies."

"Good morning," we said together.

"I have good news and bad news," the detective said. Good news, there are no electronic listening devices in your homes. However, we have discussed it, and are still hesitant to let you go back. It's all too clear this person, or persons are very dangerous."

Our faces fell like a half-baked cake.

"Now wait, ladies, he said, seeing our disappointment. We do have a plan B. It's not our favorite, but I understand you would rather be in your own space. The only reason we are willing to consider this is because you have some experience in self-protection, and the use of a firearm, Mrs. Greenly. Do you feel comfortable with that responsibility?"

His eyes met mine with the question.

"Only if Gert agrees to stay at my place, or both of us at her place."

"Mrs. Bush?"

"I guess I can do that if you think it will help."

"Good, replied the detective. We're trying to figure out how to add our people at The White Dove without it being obvious.

Mrs. Bush, if you stay with Mrs. Greenly, would you mind if we put a couple of female officers in your place? We could pass them off as family, or friends of the family visiting for a few days. You could say you are staying with Mrs. Greenly to give them room at your place. Would that work for you?"

"One of them would have to sleep on the couch," answered Gert.

"Not a problem. They will be taking turns watching for anything suspicious at night anyway. They can see Mrs. Greenly's place from yours, so that works. I'll leave it to you to come up with the details of who they are, their relationship, etc. You'll be able to remember it better that way."

"Do we get to go home now?" I asked, hoping like hell he was going to say, "Yes."

"It is going to take at least a couple of hours to get this all set up. How about I give you a call when things are in place. You'll need to sign the officers in as your guests, so we'll set up a place for you to meet them. If you want to get your things together, you'll be ready to leave when I call."

"Would it be okay, since we'll be leaving soon anyway, if we go out for lunch on our own?" I asked. "We will watch carefully to make sure no one is following us."

"I guess, but be extremely vigilant, and stay away from the mall and the hospital. Call me immediately if you suspect a problem. Oh, that reminds me: the bad news. Eddie has pneumonia. He's been moved to Intensive Care. You won't be able to see him today. It may be a day or two. Even then, I don't want you going to the hospital without a plan and some assistance. Do you have your gun with you, or is it at home?"

"I've had it with me since Eddie's fall," I answered.

Gert flashed me a raised eyebrow of concern, but she didn't say anything.

"Good for you," he said, with a smile. "I'd better get going and get the arrangements made."

"Oh, we did find out Eddie's brother was a judge. You probably already know that," I added.

"Yes. We found he was a judge, and his wife died two years before him. Don't know if that helps us any. I'm still not sure Eddie was talking about his brother, but we'll continue to check him out. Remember, I can't tell you all the details of our investigation."

"We appreciate what you've told us," I answered. I wanted to say: We already know about his wife from Neal's obituary. We're doing pretty well on our own, thank you. But I managed to keep my big mouth, respectfully shut. After all, he had been good to us, and I didn't want him to discover what we were doing behind his back...slippery slope.

"I'll call later," he said. "Have a good lunch, and be extra careful." He waved as he hurried out the door.

Gert and I gathered up our meager belongings. It was tempting to leave the wig, and the rest of the gaudy disguise, but who knows. One can never tell what one might need. After all, they did get us out of the White Dove.

Chapter 22

We said our goodbyes to Officer Flynn and backed out of the driveway. Although it had been a short time, it felt as if we had been cooped up for weeks. Hallelujah! We were free.

"Where shall we go to celebrate?" I asked, as our wheels rolled onto the street.

"We could try a tea room. They always have such a cozy feeling. We could use a soothing atmosphere for a change," Gert offered.

"Sounds perfect. How about the new one on Commercial Street?"

"Great choice. Here we go," she said, looking like a bird released from a cage.

We smiled all the way across town. It's not like we had been in prison, but being restricted is not pleasant for most people. I smiled at the thought of how constrained the damn person responsible for this was going to be when we caught him. I thought "we" because it was now imbedded in my mind that Gert and I would solve this evil nightmare, and the possibility of Niger having a hand in it was not an option.

We parked in front of the tearoom with its lacy curtains and generous display of antiques. Fluffy clouds drifted overhead, and the smell of freshly baked quiche lured us like a baby toward a pacifier.

Inside we were seated at a table in the rear of the dining room. There was only one other occupied table. The room was covered with antique lamps, quilts, teapots, and hundreds of other charming pieces from the past. It was impossible to take it all in. If the aromas drifting from the kitchen were an example of what was to come, we had hit the jackpot.

"Oh my. This is a lovely place. I'm really anxious to try the food," said Gert, with a smile that was almost a drool.

"Me too."

A young girl came over with a small dish of dainty muffins, and offered us a choice of flavored iced teas, coffee or water with lemon. She handed us menus, took our drink orders, and left us to peruse the yummy choices offered.

"Looks like we got here at the right time." Several small groups were now waiting to be seated.

"We sure did," Gert agreed.

After careful consideration of the menu, we made our choices and placed our orders.

"Guess we'd better give some thought to your new tenants."

"You're right. We don't really have a lot of time to work this out. It has to sound reasonable. Could we say they were my nieces, or maybe Janet's sorority sisters who wanted to visit Branson and the Ozarks?"

"I think the sorority sisters is a great idea. The relative idea could get complicated if people asked too many questions, and we don't all give the same answers. Super idea, Gert. We will have to sign them in with last names, but first names should be enough for introductions, since you won't be expected to know them that well."

We choose Sarah and Angel, and decided to let the rest fall as it may. Our food arrived, and we were ready to relax and enjoy. The place was packed by now. The food was delicious.

"Oh, holy hell! Gert, look who just walked in. Careful. Hunch down as much as you can."

Gert took a quick peek, and turned as white as her napkin.

Standing near the door, talking to the hostess were Mr. Bennett and Mabel.

For the most part, Gert's back was toward them. I put a napkin up to my face, and wished for once that my hair were brown instead of red.

We watched as best we could. The hostess seated them in a tall, secluded corner booth near the front of the room: Bennett's pick. Perhaps he didn't want to be seen either.

"How are we going to get out of here?" Gert asked, in a panicked tone.

There was a large antique lamp between the offensive booth and me. I was partially hidden and only Mabel's lap and legs were visible. Thankfully, Mr. Bennett's back was toward us. This was fine now, but if we tried to leave, he would have a perfect view of us going out the door.

"Hell, Gert! It just dawned on me. We don't have to worry about them seeing us. We just have to make them think we didn't see them."

"Oh, true. We have a perfect right to be here. It's them that have some explaining to do."

Each of us heaved a big sigh of relief as our waitress offered an assortment of deserts. We declined on the sweets, paid our bills, and planned our escape route.

Outside the dining area was an extensive assortment of antique dishes, clothing, slippers, candles and a million other things. Standing, we pretended to inspect a set of small teacups just beyond the tables. Our backs were to the offending couple. Without looking toward the front door, or the repellant booth, we meandered to the far side of the store and looked at scarves, candy, and various antiques: all the while making our way toward the door.

As we left the old building, it was tempting to make a break for the car, but walk we must.

"Oh, damn! That was too close for comfort. There is sure as hell something going on between those two. Mabel, I was already wondering about, but Mr. Bennett is a shock. Maybe it's just an affair of sorts, but somehow I don't see it that way."

"It does seem a bit off," Gert replied. "But everything does at this point."

Gert had started the car and was backing out.

"Let's move the car. Make it look like we're leaving, but find a spot where we can see them come out. It may not tell us anything, but I'd like to see how they act and if they came together."

Gert circled the block, and found a parking place in an alley near one of the many antique shops. We hopped out and entered the store through a side door. A clerk asked if he could help us. We said we were just looking, and headed for the front where we had a wonderful view of the tearoom across the street.

We were feeling a bit conspicuous after picking over the same objects repeatedly for ten minutes. Thankfully, the door across the street opened and our suspicious couple strolled out. They didn't seem concerned or nervous. I felt sure they hadn't seen us at all. Must have been an intense conversation…?

They both walked to the driver's side of a blue Ford. They appeared to say a few words. Mabel had a serious, not very happy look on her face. If this was an affair, it didn't seem to be going well. She got in the car and started it up. Mr. Bennett walked to a white SUV, and climbed inside. Both cars backed out: heading in opposite directions.

Strange.

Gert and I headed for the side door. Outside, we climbed in her car and sat thinking for a few seconds.

"We can't follow either of them. They both know my car," said Gert.

"That's okay. We saw what we needed to see."

"Yes, but I wish we knew what it meant."

Chapter 23

Mozart leapt to life in my purse.

"Hello."

"Detective Lancaster here. Did you have a good lunch?"

"Fantastic."

"We have a meeting arranged at Big Mona's on Commercial St. Do you know where that is?"

I almost dropped my phone. We were sitting practically across from the place. Something held me from offering that information.

"Yes, I've been there," I said.

"Good. We thought it would be best to meet someplace not so close to the White Dove."

You and apparently everyone else, I thought.

"The officers will be dressed in jeans, and one will be wearing three turquoise bracelets, so you can recognize them. They'll make sure they're sitting at a table for four. Have you thought of any ideas for a cover story?"

"Yes. Gert is going to introduce them as two of her daughter, Janet's, sorority sisters. They will be staying with her so they can visit Branson and other attractions in the Ozarks."

"Great idea. I knew I could depend on you two."

A smile of satisfaction found my lips. A little praise feels mighty good. I'd pass it along to the one who deserved it.

"The ladies should be there in fifteen minutes. Will that give you enough time?"

"Oh, sure. That should be fine," I answered, feeling a slight twinge of guilt. Technically it wasn't a lie, but I seemed to be stretching the truth a lot lately.

"I'll touch base later to see how things are going, and will let you know how Eddie is doing. Poor guy. I sure hope he pulls through this. He might know something that could break this case open. Talk later," he said, and hung up.

His last words left me feeling a bit down. Eddie was in bad shape. Guilt washed over me at the thought of how rude I had been five minutes before he tripped, slipped or was pushed down those stairs. Now he had become a friend, and important. I had to shake it off if I was going to get to the bottom of this ungodly mess.

I still couldn't figure out how someone had managed to push him, and I felt they had, and then disappear before we came out of the snack room. The only things at the top of the stairs were the restrooms, a hall to the library, and the one we came down. Not many places to hide, but it seemed someone had managed to stay out of sight.

I smiled, and turned to Gert. "The detective really likes your idea about Janet's friends.

Gert grinned. I could see she was pleased to get some credit for our investigation. I realized again how important she was to me, and how seldom I expressed my appreciation. That had to change.

"We're supposed to meet them at Big Mona's in fifteen minutes. Want to just sit here a few minutes, since we're so close already?"

"Sure. I'll put the windows down so we can enjoy the breeze."

Puffy little clouds drifted peacefully across the sky. Small groups of people came and went, as they strolled by smiling and chatting going to or from lunch, perhaps. It was a stark contrast to the thoughts stomping like war bound medieval soldiers through our heads.

"I'm so glad you spotted the snake pin in that picture. That was a tremendous find. Great job, Gert."

"Pure luck," she replied modestly.

"Well, it sure as hell gave us direction, which was way more than we had before."

We sat thinking in silence a bit more, and then decided we should head for our rendezvous with our undercover ladies.

Gert moved her car about half a block, and we walked a short distance to the coffee shop. The lunch hour being pretty much over, it was not at all crowded. There were a few tables in the front where orders are placed. A young man with a computer occupied one. The others were empty. We placed requests for a mocha latte and a peach tea. We headed toward an opening into a back room that contained a few more tables.

'Three blue bracelets' was waiting for us with her friend. They both looked like college kids instead of police officers. Seemed to be a theme.

The timing had worked like a charm. No one else was in the room.

"Hello," said bracelet girl. "You must be Joyce and Gertrude," she said, with a big smile as she pulled chairs out for us.

"That would be us," I answered. Gert and I sat down. "I'm Joyce and this is Gertrude."

"Nice to meet you," they replied, each shaking our hands.

"I'm whomever you want me to be," said Bracelet Girl, as she sat back down.

The other girl said, "Me too," adding, "It will be less confusing if we just use the names you have decided on, rather than you trying to remember both and keep them straight."

"Good idea. We decided to call you Sarah and Angel, if that's good for you."

"Perfect," said the second girl. "I have a sister named Sarah, so I'll take that one."

Our drinks arrived.

"Iced tea?" the girl asked.

"That's me," Gert replied.

"I guess the latte is for you then," our waitress said, as she sat the drinks in their respective places. "Can I get you anything else?"

"No, thanks," I said, looking at Gert who nodded her head in agreement.

Alone again, we continued our conversation with 'Sarah' and 'Angel.'

It was decided that they were both from Des Moines, IA, since they were each somewhat familiar with the city. Doubtful, but someone might ask questions. We picked Alpha Chi Omega, as that had actually been Janet's sorority. Since we were not pretending to know them well ourselves, it wasn't necessary to have a great deal of knowledge.

We finished our drinks, and were soon on our way to the White Dove, with the officer's following in a plain car. Gert and I were planning to cover our absence, if necessary, with a night in Eureka Springs, AR. This was only if someone actually noticed we hadn't been in our cabins, which was doubtful, especially with the supposed TV man calling on us yesterday.

We decided to leave our things in the car until later when we could maybe sneak them in without being noticed. Since we hadn't signed out, we had Sarah and Angel Park a block away, and give us time to sneak into the snack room. They were to follow in thirty minutes and have Gertrude paged. We would go to the lobby, greet them and get each signed in as a visitor.

It is hard to hold your breath, and try to look casual. We did our best. One of the ladies who uses a rather complicated walker, and a woman we assumed to be her daughter, were standing at the book which keeps track of our comings and goings. Thank God! It gave us a perfect opportunity to stroll by without taking a second look.

We were sitting in the snack room, sipping glasses of water, when the page came through that Gertrude was needed at the front desk. We had heard the visitor's buzzer go off a couple of minutes before.

It went down smooth as a baby's butt. Gert greeted them with hugs, and introduced them to me. We got them signed in, and were in Gertrude's place within ten minutes.

Wow! What a relief.

Chapter 24

After a quick tour of the place, and an exchange of phone numbers, Gert packed a change of clothes, and PJ's in a grocery bag, and we headed to my place. Sarah and Angel watched to see which cabin was mine.

"Now what?" Gertrude asked, as she plopped on the sofa, which would be her bed tonight, and maybe more.

"We have to get back to our investigation, and that means we need to get our laptops out of your car. We've lost several hours, and I wanted this over like yesterday."

"Me too. You wait here and I'll go to my car and get both of our computers. Give me a grocery bag. I think they'll both fit."

"Here, I've got a Penney's shopping bag. That should do the trick. You might want to put some of your clothing over them, so they're not so obvious. Don't worry about any of my things. We will have to get all of it eventually, but right now I'm not in the mood to see that hideous yellow dress."

Gert took the bag and went out the door, saying she would she would be right back. The minute she stepped off the porch, I felt prickles of fear walking up my spine. Where the hell did that come from? I asked myself. She's only going to the parking lot in broad daylight. But I couldn't shake it. I stood on the porch waiting: all sorts of things running through my head.

I was still standing on the porch when I heard the faint sound of my phone. Hurrying inside, I grabbed it and answered. "Hello."

"Call Detective Lancaster, and get Sarah and Angel out here," Gertrude gasped.

"What, what's going on?"

"Just get out here," she shouted, and hung up.

My knees were so weak; it took wasted seconds to get my feet moving. I ran for the door, my chest throbbing with fear for Gertrude. Somehow I managed to hit speed-dial for Det. Lancaster. I yelled, "Get to the White Dove as fast as you can and hung up."

My Glock was in my pocket, but I felt it better not to tear through the yard with it in view until I saw if it was needed.

I reached Gert's cabin huffing and panting, and dragged our undercover protectors out the door, by yelling, "Gert's in danger." We ran like wild people toward the front door. None of us had a clue why: except Gert had told us to.

We rounded the corner into the front lobby, and saw Gert leaning against the table, looking pale and frightened. Wisely, she motioned us outside, rather than causing a ruckus inside. We still had no idea why we were following her through the parking lot. Since our protectors were undercover, they could not take charge unless it was a life or death situation.

Gert stopped about ten feet from her car and pointed toward

her windshield.

The three of us crept forward and stared at the grotesque warning. It made my blood run cold. This was personal. This was evil.

A dead bird, its head separated from its body, was lying on the windshield: a smear of blood between the body parts. Near the bird, and under her wiper blade, was a note. We looked through the driver's side glass, and read it: one word: "STOP" in bright red, and all caps.

Gert explained she had felt so threatened when she saw the grotesque sight; she stood frozen for a few seconds. Then forgetting all about her errand, she dropped the bag, and ran back to the building. She grabbed the phone on the sign-in table when she came though the entryway and we knew the rest.

Sarah pulled her phone from her jacket. Between huffs, and pants, running to find Gert, I told her I had called Det. Lancaster. She now called him and explained what had actually happened. It was decided he would come in quietly, with no siren under the circumstances. He would call a lab guy to meet him. It would be best if we caused as little commotion as possible.

We did our best to act as if we were having a normal, friendly conversation until they got there.

When the detective and lab guy arrived, Lancaster told us to go back to Gert's cabin, and try to act as if nothing much had happened. "Stay together until you hear from me."

"Can we get our computers and things out of the car?" I asked.

"Yes, that would be fine. It doesn't look as if anyone's been in the car. Let me open the door with gloves, just in case someone checked to see if it was unlocked. I'll hand your things out to you."

This event scared the crap out of me, but also made me angry as hell, and even more determined to track the malicious killer down.

As we gathered up our things, I noticed Sam Johnson, a resident, getting out of a cab. He walked a few steps toward us, and I'm pretty sure he could see the bird, probably not much more.

"Hi, Sam. How are you doing?" I asked, placing myself between him and Gert's car.

"Just got back from an eye appointment. What's going on?"

"Oh, we think a hawk, or some bird of prey, just dropped his lunch on Gert's car. I have a friend that was driving down a country road near Ozark, and a hawk dropped a mouse on the hood of her car. The mouse was alive. Our bird didn't have the same luck. Or it could have been a small boy with a new BB gun. Who knows?" I said, with what I hoped was a convincing grin.

"Why the police cars over a dead bird?" Sam asked.

"Oh, they had just stopped by to ask us something else.

They happened to get here about the time we saw the bird. You know how touchy things are with all that's happened around here, so they take a good look at everything." I gave a slight dismissive wave, and said. "See you at supper, Sam."

The four of us women headed toward the building. Sam glanced briefly at the car, and followed.

As we came in, Big Jim Landis was coming out. Damn, I had to find a way to get some more info on him. If anyone had the size to kill Jake and put him in the Gazebo, he fit the bill.

I still couldn't get over him watching us with Jake's body. He seemed to always be around. Could he have been responsible for the bird?

We headed toward Gert's place with our arms full. This was not at all the lighthearted event I had described to Sam. It was serious: dead serious.

"How did you come up with that story so fast?" Sarah questioned.

"Because the part about the hawk and the mouse was true. It just popped into my head at the right time. It wasn't hard to arrange it to fit our situation. I was pretty sure he wasn't close enough to see the note. So we lucked out on that one."

"Good job," Angel, chimed in.

Inside Gert's place, we sorted our things from the car. Gertrude took her dirty clothes out of the Penney's bag and put them in the hamper. We headed back toward my place with our laptops under our arms. I noticed Nora's curtain move, so I gave a wave in her direction. I would try and give her a call later.

As we entered my cabin, I turned to Gert. "Would you like to take your turn in the shower now, or wait until after we get back from dinner?"

"Go ahead if you want. I'm still a bit rattled. I think I just want to relax for a bit. Do you mind if I fix myself a cup of tea?"

"Certainly not. Help yourself. I'll take my turn then. I hope a good hot shower will get me back on track." I grabbed some clean clothes, and moved toward the bathroom. Gert headed to the kitchen.

We had arranged to go by and pick up our sorority girls at 5:30 for dinner. This had been such a weird day. I wasn't sure I wanted to eat. I was more into 'thinking mode'.

The girls were ready when we stopped by to get them. They were each wearing jeans. Sarah had a light cotton jacket covering a print top. Angel wore a red top with a denim jacket. They looked young, attractive and relaxed. Gert and I were less calm. We knew their jackets covered firearms. To be truthful, my Glock was in my purse, so I probably felt less tense than Gertrude.

Several faces, displaying question marks, looked up as we entered. This was to be expected as new young faces always drew interest. Since Nora was having her food delivered, I wondered who would be the first to approach with questions.

We made it through the buffet, and were seated before the first contact came. It was Mabel.

"Lovely, are these your daughters?" she asked, looking from my face to Gert's.

"No, but we would take them," Gert said, with a sweet smile. "They are two of my daughter Janet's sorority sisters. This is Sarah, and this is Angel. They are here to visit Branson and other parts of the Ozarks."

"Janet has told us so much about the area, we thought we just had to see it for ourselves," explained Angel.

"Well, she was right," said Mabel. "I'm a transplant myself, and I love it here. I'll move on though and let you eat. It was so nice to meet you."

They exchanged smiles, and she moved across the room to sit with three other residents.

Most people now turned to each other, or their own plates. They knew that the information about the visitors would slide around the room and eventually reach their ears.

The girls seemed to enjoy the food, and were impressed that we had such quality meals. We were lucky. We knew that, but Gert and I, even though we managed to keep up some semblance of normal conversation and eat a bit, were not enjoying it as much as we usually did. All we could think about were the secrets hiding in our computers, and the information in Eddie's head that we might never get.

After finishing our meal, I suggested we wrap some cookies

in paper napkins in case we wanted a snack later. Sarah and Angel did the same.

Chapter 25

Gert and I were finally alone in my cabin. I gave her my Wi-Fi password, and we settled down. I wanted to find more on the Rossi family. Gert was going to work on the trial information.

Our digging was much more difficult than it sounds. Just one word in a search can head you in a direction that is not at all what you're looking for. About nine o'clock, not even sure how I got there, I came across an article about Tony, Jr.'s half-brother, Henry, having disappeared. He was never found. Foul play was suspected, but nothing ever turned up. They had never even had a suspect. Another interesting fact was that his last name was not Rossi. It was Anderson. It had been swimming around in my subconscious, but I just now realized Helen and Henry were probably not Italian. Their names were not the usual names seen in people of that nationality. I was not sure if this was significant or not. It could explain why there were so few Rossi's in Wilmington. Italians are usually a pretty tight knit group. Maybe the Rossi family didn't like Helen, or wanted Anthony Sr. to marry someone else.

It also explained why Tony was named Junior, even though he was not the oldest son. Henry was not Anthony's son, and his stepfather never adopted him. Why?

At the bottom of the article it mentioned how close the

brothers were, and stated Henry had just graduated from the University of Delaware when he disappeared. Junior was heartbroken when Henry vanished.

On a whim, I pulled up information on the university's graduating class for that year. There he was near the top of the page. He had a BA in Gerontology. That was not what I was expecting, or that he looked slightly familiar. Of course he had a mullet like most young men of that era. That tended to make them all look somewhat alike.

I stared at the page for several minutes, looking for I don't know what, when my eyes caught another degree in gerontology. A shock wave almost threw me off my seat at the table. The name beside this degree was Scott Bennett, the same as our director! But this Scott Bennett was black. What the hell!

"Gert, look at this. This is just too weird. Something stinks to high heaven. This can't be a coincidence."

After more searching we found that there seemed to be two Scott Bennetts. The African American one died in a car accident a couple of months after his smiling graduation picture had been posted. Another Scott Bennett held part ownership in a few businesses in Branson. One was a retirement center that he owned entirely.

Twelve thirty found us dressed in all black, and sneaking out my back door, with our phones on vibrate. Gert had to roll up the sleeves of a sweatshirt I had loaned her. We hadn't planned for this outing.

We should have contacted Sarah and Angel, but what if we were wrong? Our pride was so encompassing neither of us could stand the vision of Niger smirking at us as if we were 'dried up old fools'.

We crept like large spiders along the back of each cabin. As we passed Nora's, I could only think how horrified she would be if we made a noise, and she saw us. We couldn't let that happen. Past the next cabin, we had no choice except to drop to our knees and crawl. Thankfully, there were some shrubs tall enough to cover our approach to the main building. The sliding doors to this building were locked after midnight, but were lit by large bulbs that came on at dusk.

Chapter 26

"Angel, get up. I think I just saw a shadow moving behind Joyce's place!" yelled Sarah, as she stared between the curtains.

Angel, fully dressed, stood by her side within seconds. If they got any sleep on assignments like this, they had to leave their clothes on, just in case. "Let's try calling to warn them."

Sarah grabbed her phone and tried both numbers: straight to voicemail on both. "Let's get over there. Something's not right, unless they turned their phones off so they could get some sleep."

"I can't see them doing that. They'd want us to be able to get ahold of them if necessary," she said, as she opened the door.

Not knowing what the shadow was, the two officers crept toward Joyce's cabin. Using small trees and shrubs, they worked their way across the lawn. It was a slow process. If one of the tenants saw them, and reported them, it would probably cause a major uproar. They would have trouble explaining their actions without revealing who they were.

When they reached the door, Sarah knocked, lightly. No response. She knocked with more force. When no one came to the door, she took the key Joyce had loaned her, and opened the door. It was pitch dark, except for a small nightlight. Even in the dim light, it was obvious the open floor plan cottage was empty.

"Oh, hell. Where are they?" whispered Angel. "Did they sneak out on their own, or did someone take them?"

"I don't have a clue, but I now know for sure that I did see someone. We've got to find them. I've never lost anyone on my watch, and I'm not starting now," Sarah said, a determined tone in her voice. Let's look out back. What I saw was behind, and between, the cabins."

Guns in hand, the officers crept through the back door. They had to be prepared for anything. Why in the world would the women sneak out without telling them? Sarah felt sure they had a good relationship with the ladies. Wouldn't they have asked for their help if they were in danger? This scared her. Maybe they had not been able to call them.

Angel's head was filled with who could have taken them. Was it the same person who put the bird and note on the windshield? They had to be cautious. She liked these ladies, and certainly didn't want anything to happen to them.

They silently inched their way behind, bushes, cabins and trees. Whispering was not an option now. It was impossible to know what was in the shadows, behind a bush, or lying in wait at the corner of a cottage. Since the shadow Sarah had seen seemed to be going toward the main building, they did the same.

Chapter 27

We prayed Sarah or Angel had not caught a glimpse of our shadowy bodies and come to investigate.

Thank the Lord; I still had a way to get in the building without going through the front door. Fannie had given me a key to the barely visible door on the side of the building, when I was working on the case for her brother. She probably forgot all about it, but not me, and I was very thankful now.

We crawled to the edge of the sidewalk. This door was pretty much blocked from view by a tree near the end of the shrubs, and an enormous pot of begonias. It was unlikely anyone in the cabins could see us. We stood and scurried across the sidewalk. The keyhole was barely visible, but after a couple of tries, I managed to get the key in the slot.

Now came the scary part. The building was locked, but two attendants worked in the office at night. If someone had an emergency, they could call the office and someone would come help them or call for emergency backup. It was impossible to know where the night people were at this moment. If they had to use the bathroom, or stretch their legs, we could walk right into them. It's not like they were going to shoot us, but we would have some serious explaining to do.

"Here goes," I whispered to my partner.

The door opened easily, with very little noise. But we were

hypersensitive at this moment, so it sounded like The Gong Show.

We stood like statues for about thirty seconds, peeping through a half-inch opening. There was nothing but muted darkness down the hallway. A glow at the end indicated the office lights. Small security lights near the floor, lit a dim path: maybe to prevent a fall on the way to the restrooms? We stepped inside. I turned the deadbolt to make sure we couldn't be followed, just in case someone had seen us. Like shadows we crept toward the light. I wrapped my fingers around the gun in my pocket, so it wouldn't bump against the wall.

The light was much brighter as we neared the office. We could hear music that seemed to be coming from that area. It was important to know where the attendants were. Our target was Mr. Bennett's office. If the workers were both together, we could move more safely. I motioned for Gert to stay at the edge of the hallway, as I crept forward to have a peek through the glass in the workroom windows. Someone dropped what sounded like a fork. Oh, shit!

I hugged the wall for the next few seconds, willing my heart not to burst. The quiet crept on, after a slight rustle probably to retrieve the piece of silverware. I continued my way toward the window. There were boxes stacked on a shelf close to the glass. This was a big plus for me. I peeked carefully into the bright lights, and could see a male and a female sitting at separate desks, paying no attention to each other. The man was played a game on his computer, and the woman was engrossed with her cell phone and a salad. A radio, near the window, was tuned to a rock station. Perfect!

I turned to Gert and motioned for her to join me. Mr. Bennett's office was at the far end of the hall. I was thankful for the security lights. They were not very bright, but perfect for showing us where to go. They didn't attract as much attention as the little flashlight in my pocket would have.

Chapter 28

After what seemed like forever, the officers reached the side of the main building. Sarah pointed at the side door. With hand jesters, she indicated she was going to check the door. On her tummy, she slithered through the grass until the door was in reach. Rising to her knees, she carefully tried the knob. It was locked.

Angel understood her partner's disappointment, from her reaction. They weren't going in that way.

"We have no choice," Sarah whispered, as she crawled back to Angel. "We're going to have to reveal who we are and go through the front door. If someone took them, we need to sound the alarm. If they're inside, for some reason, we need to know why."

"Let me take a quick peek to see if their cars are in the lot, Sarah said, as she crawled toward the fence and the back corner of the building. Moments later she was back.

"Both their cars are there. I don't like this."

"We'd better call Det. Lancaster," whispered Angel. "I can't believe they would leave the grounds willingly on their own. Something's wrong!"

They stood. Angel made the call, and they walked to the front door. It might take a bit to explain what was going on, but they had to take charge NOW!

Chapter 29

We crept to the door. I tried the handle. Damn, double damn! It was locked. We stood a few seconds, feeling irritated, stupid and wondering what in hell to do next. Frustrated, I stuffed my hand in my left pocket. There it was; the key that got us in the side door. Couldn't hurt. I felt carefully and stuck it in the lock. I took a deep breath and turned it. Hot damn! It must be a master key. Gert grabbed my arm and gave it a squeeze of excitement.

As quickly as the joy of the key working filled us with a sense of accomplishment, a bolt of fear replaced it. What was on the other side of that door? We had a sizable stack of paper evidence that practically proved Mr. Bennett was most likely Henry Anderson, and Tony Rossi's half-brother. These were mobsters: horrible, dangerous people. We had already seen Jake's murder, and I now considered Eddie's fall an attempted murder, or possibly murder too, if he didn't make it.

My hand shook as I slowly turned the knob, and pushed the door forward. Gert's fingers were biting into my arm. I didn't mind. It told me my friend was with me, and we were still alive.

The room was not totally black. Streetlights offered a bit of light through two partially covered windows. While I appreciated the light from the windows, I also realized our flashlight would be visible to anyone outside. We needed more light than what was coming through them anyway. We had some serious searching to do. It would be best to close the heavy drapes.

"Can you close those drapes?" I said, whispering and pointing. "I'll get the ones over here, and turn on my flashlight."

As soon as we finished this task, I realized the flashlight was too small. It was still too dark. I spotted a desk light with a green shade sitting on a massive walnut desk. I reached out and pushed the switch. A warm glow filled the room, backed by menacing shadows in every corner and around each piece of furniture. Creepy as hell!

It was clear our director enjoyed luxury. The furniture was high-end, and what appeared to be beautiful, expensive paintings lined the walls. My heart skipped a beat as my flashlight fell on an extensive, pricy looking display of knives.

"Oh, hell, look at that, Gert."

"Oh, my Lord. He loves knives," she whispered, as she added more small bruises to my arm.

"This doesn't look good. Let's look in the desk, and see if we can find anything that might prove he really is Rossi's brother. We need to make this fast, and get out of here."

We each took a side of the walnut monstrosity, and dug as quietly as possible through paper, pens, clips and forms. The lower drawers held a few boxes containing awards, pen sets, and ordinary items. Gert opened the bottom drawer on her side. She pulled out a small box, held it up to the light, and said, "This one is empty."

"Wait, let me look at that," I said, taking it from her and turning my flashlight to get a better look. "Gert, look at the shape of the imprint in the bottom."

"Oh, my. The snake pin would fit perfectly!" she said, dropping the box.

As the box landed on the desk, a gold sticker flashed, 'Evans Jewelers, Wilmington, DE'.

"Can I help you ladies?"

We almost fainted. The voice was soft, and it belonged to Mr. Bennett, who now stood behind a chair…with a gun pointed at us.

We stood frozen by fear. Where in the hell did he come from? How did he get past us?

"Too bad you didn't know about the hidden door in the back of the closet, and the little cameras outside to let me know if nosey old women are crawling around." He flashed a big smile, obviously quite pleased with his position.

"I see you've found my little secret. You must have seen Tony's pin. I do so regret wearing it that night, but I wanted Jake to get the message. His words at Tony's trial were the reason he had to die. The pin was a gift from me to Tony. He loved it, and wore it every day. Jake knew it well."

He stood quite still for a few seconds: looking right through us.

I had taken my gun out of my pocket, and put it on the desk when we first started our search. It was cumbersome and bumped into the wood as I moved around. It was near a carved wooden box, which probably blocked it from Bennett's view, but could I get to it before he shot us?

He blinked, and was now staring at us: not through us.

"Well, how do you wish to die?" he chuckled. "I can always choke and stab you like Jake. That would be poetic, now wouldn't it? You two have caused me more trouble than half the people Tony and I killed. Why couldn't you just leave it alone?" he whispered in a soft menacing tone. "I told you to STOP, did I not?" His mouth turned up at the corners.

Stop? Oh, hell! The bird on the windshield! Crap! He was a master at intimidation. I shuttered to think what Jake had gone through. I realized Jake probably didn't have any idea who his attacker was until the night he was killed. Henry Anderson had disappeared years before Tony's trial. Jake only knew him as Mr. Bennett: a trustworthy administrator. How hideous to think you are safe, only to find you are in the viper's nest. Poor Jake.

"Or, I could push you down the stairs like Eddie, he continued. This time, however, I would make sure your necks were broken, like I would have done if you hadn't hovered over him like the doting mother I know you are not," he said, looking at me.

Ouch, that hurt. What did he know about my mothering skills? I love my boys. They chose to work for a company that sent them to live in France, so I don't get to see them as much as I would like. That doesn't mean I don't want to see them. I inched my fingers closer to my gun: pissed, angry, and terrified.

"Eddie was like you. Just too damn noisy; didn't know when to quit. He was poking around my nursing home in Branson. Then he started asking about Jake. Don't know how in hell he got his PI nose into the mix, but it will end badly for him. I'll get him one-way or another. He has no idea who he's messing with."

He stood for a few seconds: seemingly planning Eddie's demise. My fingers made contact with my Glock.

"Well ladies, guess I'll just have to shoot you, though I much prefer knives, but it can get complicated when there's more than one target. This is what happens when you break into places. You get shot by an innocent man protecting his property in the dark," he said, as he raised his gun.

My Glock was now in my hand, my finger on the trigger, but a shot rang out before I could pull.

We looked in amazement as Bennett's gun flew from his hand, and blood spurted from his chest.

"What the hell just happened?" I shouted, pointing my gun at what now appeared to be a dead man.

"Sorry, it had to go this far," said Mabel, stepping out of the shadows. "I couldn't let him kill my friends. It took me a few minutes to decide if I should hurt him or shoot to kill. But, I realized my husband had crossed the line long ago. He would never have stopped."

I now had my gun pointed at Mabel, but without hesitation, she pitched hers on the floor, and sat quietly in a chair: her hands in her lap. She must have known about the secret door, too.

"Call the police," she said. "It's over."

Gertrude and I came to life, still stunned, but able to move.

"I'll call Det. Lancaster, if you want to get Sarah and Angel."

Gert nodded, and we made the necessary calls, not realizing our sorority girls were already in the building: although the wrong end.

Mabel raised her head and said, "He wasn't always like this. When his mother married Anthony, Sr., Henry thought he was going to have a real father. His died when he was a baby. But for some reason, his stepfather seemed to hate him from the moment the 'I do's' were said. When Tony came along, the boys, much to their dad's dismay, were closer than regular siblings. There was nothing they wouldn't do for each other.

Unfortunately, Tony was even more evil than his father, and soon turned Henry into a monster as well." She dropped her head, and began to sob quietly.

Seeing as how she probably just saved our lives, and that

was a weighty event, I stood next to her, and thanked her for what she'd done.

Realizing, I should check on Bennett, Anderson or whom ever, I flipped on the overhead lights, and went to check on his condition. He was not breathing. His reign of terror was finally over. His brother could rot in jail with no one to care.

Just then the place exploded with people. Sarah and Angel ran in the door, guns in hand. In cop mode, they took in the surroundings. Sarah went to check the body, and Angel put cuffs on Mabel after a quick explanation from Gert.

When Det. Lancaster and other officers arrived a few minutes later, we were sitting much like ladies at a tea party…with a body as our centerpiece.

Chapter 30

Soon a forensics team was combing the White Dove, and the rest of us were at the police station. We had to explain ourselves in depth. All parties involved, were pleased it was over, but they scolded us thoroughly.

We were questioned separately, and finally all of us gathered in a large room with coffee and doughnuts. The sun was coming up.

I was pleased to see Deputy Sam Brighton there. He had just returned from Delaware where he had been going over the Rossi case to see where they could have slipped up with Jake's cover. Since their records showed Henry Anderson as a cold case, they hadn't made the connection. Neither had anyone in his office noticed the snake pin Tony wore in court. After hearing about it being found at Jake's murder scene, they did some research, and soon realized the pin belonged to Tony. He could not have it in prison, of course, so he had given it to someone to keep for him. We now knew who that someone was, and it made perfect sense.

"Hell," Deputy Brighton, said. "I tried to find Jake a safe place, and I threw him right in the fire. If only I'd known about the Branson connection, I would've sent him to Seattle, or someplace."

We all, pretty much in unison, assured him it was not his fault.

Agent Niger sat looking on, and making no comment. He only opened his mouth if absolutely necessary, and made no eye contact with Gertrude or me. He was pissed.

It was Det. Lancaster's turn.

"Mabel has been very cooperative. She knew exactly what she was getting into before she pulled the trigger, and realizes she will probably spend most, if not all, of her life in prison. She plans to plead guilty, so there won't be a trial to go through. She has given us info on other crimes where we need to take a second look. We can't punish a dead man, but maybe we'll be able to offer closure to some families."

"You ladies were right about the car accident that killed the real Scott Bennett. Mabel said it was no accident, although she didn't know about it until just last year. Also, there is a question about Anthony Sr.'s heart attack. It seems Junior may have helped him along. He hated his dad for the way he treated Henry. They truly had a very strange bond."

Deputy Brighton spoke up. "Mabel told us the senior living place her husband owns in Branson was used to launder Tony's drug money. The two planned it for years, even down to the college degree Henry would need to make it happen. They figured it would be one of the last places we would look, and they were right."

"It seems Henry was visiting a conference at the White Dove when he spotted Jake. Tony had sent him a picture of the man who was going to testify against him. Bennett wasn't even sure Jake was the one. His looks had changed since the picture. But, someone had to pay. Henry applied for the director's position a couple of months later after the previous director of the White Dove died of food poisoning. Have to wonder about that one too."

"There are still some loose ends, like how Tony got the pin and the picture to his brother, but we are working on who the connection could have been. It wasn't Mabel."

"Henry spent quite some time trying to check Jake's background. He even had Mabel work on it. He made her do a lot of things she didn't want to do."

"Finally, he determined Jake must be the one, and you know most of the rest. He killed Jake, but leaving him in his cabin wasn't good enough. He made Mabel help him drag the body to the gazebo, so more people would see him in that ghastly state. The knife was just his 'signature' statement: also his big mistake. That's probably when he lost the pin."

"What a hate-filled life," the Deputy said. "And Mabel said it was all because he just wanted to be loved. His stepfather's rejection changed his life: maybe his brother's too. It's sometimes the little things that make all the difference," he added.

"On a different note," Det. Lancaster spoke up. You two," he turned to Gert and me, just as I'd filled my mouth with a jelly donut. "You took some very big chances, especially last night, but how you came up with all the clues to a very complicated case, is truly amazing."

"They could be dead," growled Niger, who had obviously been waiting for a chance to throw in a negative comment.

"But we're not," I said with a big smile: probably framed in powdered sugar.

"Could have been," he snarled again.

"But we're not," chimed in Gert.

"Okay, let's be adults here," said Detective Lancaster.

I could see his grin, but Niger couldn't.

Deputy Brighton let out a big snort, and then giggled like a little girl. Soon, the entire room was laughing, even Sarah and Angel, though they didn't know the entire story.

Niger pulled his papers together and left the room. This brought on more laughter.

What the heck? We'd been up through a stress filled night, and we were punchy.

"Why don't we all go home and get some rest," suggested Det. Lancaster.

"I'm not sure I can sleep right now," I said. "I'm too wound up. If it's alright with you Gert, how about we go by and check on Eddie?"

"I'm exhausted, but not sleepy, so that's fine by me. He won't be under guard now will he? So I can go in?"

"You can see him. I had them pull the guard. He's safe now. Do you mind letting me know how he's doing? I'm going to be pretty busy for the next few days."

"Sure, be glad to. Think I'll call the hospital before we head that way, just to make sure he can have visitors, and get his room number if he's out of ICU." I turned to Sarah and Angel. "It was so nice meeting you."

"The pleasure was ours," Angel said. "Even if you two are a little hard to keep up with," she said, with a grin.

"You ladies are great. Would you want to meet us for lunch sometime?" asked Sarah.

"We'd love to," Gert and I said in unison. Which brought on some more giggles.

We waved goodbye, and hurried toward my car. Yes, my car. I didn't have to hide it anymore. Since we had not been on the best of terms with our protectors, or the Detective last night, Angel rode with me, and Gert went in the car with Sarah. For some reason, I think they didn't trust us not to do something else off the radar if we were allowed to be on our own. Silly people!

I called the hospital and was given a new room number, and an all clear on visitors.

This time I parked as close as possible, which is never very close unless you are lucky enough to catch someone leaving. We were not that lucky this morning.

Inside, we took the elevator up to Eddie's room. It didn't seem right that no one was outside. It was still hard to believe it was actually over.

We were shocked as we entered the room, and saw a bright-eyed Eddie lying in the bed. He would have smiled if that were possible with his jaw wired up. It was obvious he knew who we were.

"Hi, Eddie. How are you feeling?" I asked.

"Etter," he said, with a twinkle in his eyes.

"We're so glad. We were worried about you."

"Caut brthr," he said between his teeth. We could see relief in his eyes.

"Yes, without your help, it would never have happened. We got off on your brother at first, but finally found out you meant Tony Rossi's brother. You know he's dead?" I asked.

"Es."

The officer who had been guarding him must have filled him in before he left.

"Well, no more worries about him. When you get back to the White Dove, you can relax and enjoy yourself."

Eddie winked, or at least made an attempt.

"We don't want to wear you out. We'll be back soon. When you get those wires out we will swap lots of stories. By the way, Det. Lancaster asked about you. He'll probably drop by when things settle down a bit."

"So glad you're on the mend," Gert said, as we headed toward the door.

"Tinks," Eddie said as we left.

Chapter 31

We drove back to the White Dove. The night had caught up with us, along with the many stressful days since we lost Jake. I was running on fumes, and could tell Gert was in the same condition. We were dragging. It was ten-thirty. With any luck, we should be able to make it through the building without running into many people. I was so wrong! What was I thinking! There had been a murder here last night: our Director.

A million people swarmed all over the place: residents, resident family members, employees, and worst of all reporters. Oh, hell! I wanted to cry.

Thank the Lord! Fannie appeared and grabbed us.

"I need to see you for a bit. Come with me."

She led us down the hallway we had used to sneak in last night.

"I know you two must be dead on your feet. Go out this way. Get to your cabins and get some rest. Come see me tomorrow."

She opened the door and pushed us out. We walked the same path we had taken just hours before. So many things had happened since then. They were all in a black tangle hanging out in my head. I would wait until tomorrow to sort them out. It was all as thick and fuzzy as a damn ball of yarn just now.

Gert and I entered through my back door. Somehow it

seemed different; our lives were different. I sat in my favorite chair, and Gert plopped on the sofa.

"Joyce?"

"Yes."

"Do you mind if I nap here? I would rather not be alone right now."

"I'm so glad you asked, Gert. I feel pretty much the same way. I'll get you a blanket and pillow."

Five minutes later, Gert and I had slipped off our shoes, wrapped up in blankets; her on the sofa, me on my bed, and we slept like babies.

We woke up around midnight, and ate the cookies I'd wrapped in napkins the day before. They were a little dried out, but worked well with a glass of warm milk. We finished, and returned to our blankets. My phone woke us at eight-thirty.

"You girls up yet?" asked a chipper Fannie.

"What time is it?" I stammered. I could see the sun peeking through the slats in the blinds.

"Time you we're up. I'll have breakfast ready in the conference room in an hour. Come in through the side door. There are still several people waiting for your appearance, but they can wait until you've had breakfast. See you at nine-thirty," and she hung up.

Oh, hell! I felt as if I'd been in a coma for a year.

I pulled up on one elbow to see if Gert was awake. She was

peeking over the back of the sofa with bleary eyes.

"Who was that?"

"Fannie. She's serving breakfast for us in the conference room at nine-thirty."

"Gosh, I don't remember what clothes I stuffed in my bag. You want me to shower first, while you wake up?"

"Go ahead. I'll have a cup of coffee while you're getting ready. You want some tea?"

"Thanks, but I'll fix some while you're getting ready." She scurried toward the shower with her bag in tow.

I started the coffee, and headed to the closet to get my clothes, when I realize I was already dressed, except for shoes. Can't remember the last time I'd slept in my clothes. Obviously, it hadn't affected my quality of sleep. I chose a fresh outfit.

At nine-fifteen, we headed to the main building. The sun shone, birds chirped. I realized this had not been part of our world for several days.

"Wonderful day," I said to Gert, with a pat on her shoulder.

"I was just thinking the same," she said, with a big smile.

We reached the door and found it open. Assuming that meant permission to enter, we soon found the conference room: smelling mighty good. Fannie met us at the door with a joyous smile.

"Ah, ladies. Good morning. Ready for breakfast?"

We nodded.

"I wasn't sure what you would want, so we have a little of everything. Grab your plates, and help yourselves."

I don't think either of us realized until that moment how hungry we were. I scooped up biscuits and gravy, scrambled eggs, bacon, fruit and added a scone for good measure. As we sat, I noticed Gertrude's plate was as out of control as mine.

Fannie put a Danish on a small plate, grabbed a napkin, fork and a cup of coffee. She sat across from us at the end of the big conference table.

Hell, I felt a little guilty about the amount of food on my plate, compared to Fannie's, but after the first bite, I didn't give a damn.

Fannie, looked at us and said, "I'm so sorry about all you've been through, but you two need to remember, he did this to himself. It had nothing to do with you, except you proved to be smarter than him. Now Jake can rest in peace."

Gert and I griped each other's hand under the table. She had said just what we needed to hear.

Suddenly we were aware of a huge presence in the doorway. Jim Landis was standing in the door looking as if he wanted to say something. As usual, we hadn't heard him approach.

"Come on in, Jim. He wants to say a few words to you two."

Jim ducked a bit, and entered. It was obvious he was shy, and finding it hard to speak.

"Ladies," he started. "I, I feel I need to apologize to you. I'm sure I, I've made you nervous at times during this ordeal, but most of it was not my doing. Bennett, or whatever his name was, asked me do things that seemed strange, and then later I realized how bad they made me look."

"One thing he asked me to do was remove the bulb at your back door, Mrs. Bush. He said he was going to buy a yellow bug light, which he would put in later. Said you had complained about bugs flying around your back door. I don't think anyone noticed me doing it, but it made it very convenient for him to break-in after dark. If someone had seen me, I would probably have been suspect number one."

As we listened, the words sent chills down my spine. They showed even more evidence of what a devious monster we had trusted as our director.

"As for our part, we're thankful we don't have to deal with him either," I told him.

"Let me know if I can help you with anything," he said, as he ducked back through the door, and retreated down the hall.

"He's really a nice young man," Gert replied.

Fannie and I nodded in agreement.

"Now you two have to face the waiting mob," Fannie said, as she stood and flashed us a big grin.

Oh, hells, bells, I thought, but knew it had to be done.

Nora was waiting on her scooter at the door to the common room; a big smile covered her face. I gave her a hug, and Gert did the same.

"Thank you, thank you," Nora blurted. "I feel like I've been released from a cage. You two did this, and I can't tell you how good it feels to no longer be afraid, and best of all to have friends!" She was beaming.

I was happy for her.

We made it through the crowd as soon as we could; not being rude, but we kept the answers as short as possible. An hour later, we reached the sliding glass doors, and made our exit. We started down the walk, and stopped where the sidewalk split.

"I think I'm going to call Janet and see how she would feel about me coming up for a couple of weeks," Gertrude said.

"That's great, and I'm going to call and book a flight to France."

We gave each other a big hug, and Gert said, "See you in two weeks, boss."

ABOUT THE AUTHOR

Betty Inman Shortt is an award winning author, honors graduate from Missouri State University, a retired high school English teacher, and native of southwest Missouri.

Betty was born in Sparta, MO, where she and her twin sister grew up on a dairy farm.

She loves to read, write, travel, volunteer, and enjoy family and friends. She thrives on mystery, humor and intrigue. Her iPad is filled with books that meet that need.

Her son, daughter, and two granddaughters are her pride and joy. Her first book, *The Weird Adventure of the Inman Twins,* was inspired by her desire to share her childhood with Ava and Maggie, her granddaughters.

Find more about Betty at her website:
http://bettyinmanshortt.com